finlay 6

Flashing Special

Goosebumps

Flashing Special

Chicken, Chicken
Don't Go To Sleep!
The Blob That Ate Everyone

R.L. Stine

Hippo

Scholastic Children's Books,
Commonwealth House, 1–19 New Oxford Street, London WC1A 1NU, UK
a division of Scholastic Ltd
London ~ New York ~ Toronto ~ Sydney ~ Auckland

Chicken, Chicken
Don't Go To Sleep!
The Blob That Ate Everyone
First published in the USA by Scholastic Inc., 1997
First published in the UK as *Goosebumps Flashing Special*
by Scholastic Ltd, 1997

ISBN 0 590 19730 4

Typeset by Rowland Phototypesetting Ltd, Bury St Edmunds, Suffolk

Printed and bound in China

10 9 8 7 6 5 4 3 2

CONTENTS

Goosebumps

Chicken, Chicken

I hate chickens.

They are filthy creatures, and they smell like
. . . like . . . chickens.

"Crystal, it's your turn to feed the chickens,"
Mum says. My least favourite words.

I carry the seed bucket out to the backyard,
and they come scurrying over, clucking and
squawking and flapping their greasy wings. I
hate the way they brush up against my legs as
they peck the seeds off the ground. Their
feathers are so rough and scratchy.

My brother, Cole, and I are always trying to
convince my parents to get rid of the chickens.
"Just because we live on a farm doesn't mean
we have to have chickens," I always say.

"Right! We're not farmers!" Cole agrees. "So
why do we have to have those smelly chickens?"

"It's always been our dream," Mum always
replies. Blah blah blah.

Cole and I have heard the dream story a thousand times.

3

We've heard how Mum and Dad grew up in the Bronx in New York City. How they hated the noise and the dirt and the concrete. How they dreamed of leaving the city for good and living on a farm near a small country town.

So, when Cole was two and I was four, we moved to Goshen Falls. Lucky us! The whole town is three blocks long. We have a cute little farm with a cute little farmhouse. And even though Mum and Dad are computer programmers—not farmers—we have a backyard full of chickens.

Cluck. Cluck. That's *their* dream.

My dream is that Cole gets punished for mouthing off the way he always does. And his punishment is that *he* has to feed the chickens for the rest of his life.

Everyone has to have a dream—right?

"OWW!" A chicken pecked my ankle. That hurt! Their beaks are so sharp.

I tossed a final handful of seed on the ground and hopped backwards, away from the disgusting, clucking creatures. Their little black eyes glinted in the sunlight as they strutted over the grass. Pecking each other. Bumping each other out of the way as they dipped their scrawny heads for the food.

I dropped the bucket in the back of the little barn we also use as a garage. Then I washed

4

my hands under the cold water tap at the side of the barn.

I heard a low roar. A shadow rolled over the barn. I gazed up to see a small plane dipping under the puffy afternoon clouds.

I took a deep breath. The tangy aroma of potatoes floated in the air.

That's what the farmers grow around here. Mostly potatoes and corn.

I dried my hands on the legs of my jeans and hurried off in search of my brother. It was a sunny Saturday afternoon. Most of my friends from school were away on a 4-H club trip.

Mum asked me to keep an eye on Cole. He's ten, two years younger than me. But sometimes he acts like a four-year-old. It seems like he's always finding new ways to get into trouble.

I wandered through town. No sign of him. I asked Mrs Wagner at the bakery if she'd seen him. Cole likes to stop in there and beg her for free doughnuts.

Mrs Wagner said she'd seen Cole and his friend Anthony heading out of town in the direction of Pullman's Pond.

Uh-oh, I thought. What are they planning to do at the pond? I started to the door.

"I just love your hair, Crystal," Mrs Wagner called. "It's such a beautiful deep shade of red. You should be a model. Really. You're so tall and thin."

"Thanks, Mrs Wagner!" I called as the door closed behind me. I wasn't thinking about my hair or being a model. I was thinking about Cole and Anthony and the pond.

I trotted the rest of the way through town. Waved to Mr Porter standing in the window of the Pick 'n' Pay. Then I turned off the street and followed the dirt path that led to Pullman's Pond.

I didn't have to go far to find Cole and Anthony. They were hiding behind the long hedge at the edge of Vanessa's property.

I gazed beyond the hedge to the falling-down old farmhouse where Vanessa lives.

Who is Vanessa? I guess you might say she is the most interesting person in Goshen Falls. And the most weird.

Actually, Vanessa is like someone from a horror film. She is pretty, with long, straight black hair and a pale, white face. She dresses all in black. She wears black lipstick and black fingernail polish.

Vanessa is a mystery woman. No one knows if she's young or old.

She keeps to herself. I've hardly ever seen her in town. She lives in her old farmhouse right outside of town with her black cat.

Naturally, everyone says she is some kind of sorceress.

I've heard all kinds of stories about Vanessa.

Frightening stories. Most of the kids in Goshen Falls are scared of her. But that doesn't stop them from playing tricks on her.

Kids are always daring each other to sneak up to Vanessa's house. It's kind of a game everyone plays. Sneak up to her house, tap on the window, make her cat screech. Then run away before Vanessa sees you.

"Hey—Cole!" I called in a loud whisper. I ducked my head as I ran along the hedge. If Vanessa was home, I didn't want her to see me.

"Hey, Cole—what's up?"

As I came nearer, I saw that Cole and Anthony weren't alone. Two other kids huddled behind the hedge. Franny Jowett and Jeremy Garth.

Cole raised a finger to his lips. "Ssshhhh. Vanessa is in there."

"What are you doing?" I demanded. I saw that Franny and Jeremy held plastic water jugs in their hands. "Is that lemonade or something?"

They shook their heads solemnly.

"Some kids dared them to fill Vanessa's mailbox with water," Cole explained.

"Huh?" I gasped. I stared at Franny and Jeremy. "You're not going to do it—are you?"

"They have to," Cole answered for them. "A dare is a dare."

"But that's so mean!" I protested.

My brother sniggered. "The mailbox is right

next to the front door. No way they won't get caught."

Franny and Jeremy are blond and pale. Now they looked even paler than usual. Jeremy made a soft, choking sound. Franny gripped her jug tightly and peered over the hedge at the black metal mailbox on its tilted pole.

"You accepted the dare. Are you going to wimp out?" Cole demanded.

Franny and Jeremy glanced at each other nervously. They didn't reply.

"Don't do it," Anthony suddenly chimed in.

We all turned to Anthony. He's short and chubby and has a round face and very short black hair. He wears red-framed glasses that are always slipping down his little pug nose.

"Don't do it," Anthony repeated.

"Why n-not?" Franny stammered.

"Didn't you hear what happened when Vanessa caught Tommy Pottridge?" Anthony asked in a hushed whisper. "Didn't you hear what she did to him?"

"No!" Franny and Jeremy declared together.

I felt a tremble of fear run down my back. "What did Vanessa do to Tommy?" I demanded.

I peered over the tall hedge. Did something move in Vanessa's front window?

No. Just a glint of sunlight on the windowpane.

We huddled closer to Anthony. Even though it was a warm spring day, I suddenly felt chilled. "What did Vanessa do to Tommy?" I repeated in a whisper.

"She caught him sneaking up to her house," Anthony reported. "She did some kind of magic spell on him. She made his head blow up like a balloon."

"Oh, come on!" I exclaimed, rolling my eyes.

"No—really!" Anthony protested. "His head was huge. And it got all soft and squishy. Like a sponge."

Cole laughed.

Anthony clamped a hand over Cole's mouth. "It's true!" he insisted. "Vanessa gave him a big, soft, spongy head. That's why we don't see Tommy around any more!"

"But the Pottridges moved away!" Franny cried.

"That's why they moved," Anthony replied. "Because of Tommy's head."

We all froze for a moment, thinking about Anthony's story. I tried to picture Tommy with a big, squishy head.

Cole broke the silence. "Give me that!" he cried. He grabbed the water jug from Jeremy's hands. "*I'll* fill up her mailbox. I'm not scared."

"No way!" Jeremy protested. He wrestled the jug away from my brother. Then he turned to Franny. "We're doing it—right? We were dared, so we have to do it—right?"

Franny swallowed hard. "I guess," she choked out.

"All right!" Cole cheered, slapping them both on the back. Franny nearly dropped her jug. "You can do it! Lots of kids play tricks on Vanessa. And they don't get squishy heads."

"I still think it's mean to fill someone's mailbox with water," I protested. "And it's not worth the risk."

No one wanted to listen to me or my warnings.

Franny and Jeremy tiptoed to the end of the hedge. Then they began slowly making their way over the tall, weed-choked grass.

They carried their plastic water jugs in both hands in front of them. And they kept their eyes on the tilted mailbox to the right of the front door of Vanessa's farmhouse.

Cole, Anthony and I crept out from behind the hedge to watch. I held my breath and stared at the front window, looking for Vanessa.

But the glare of yellow sunlight filled the windowpane. I couldn't see a thing.

Franny and Jeremy seemed to be moving in slow motion. It was taking them *forever* to cross the lawn to the mailbox!

A million tiny white gnats flew over the tall grass. Swirling and dancing in the sunlight, the gnats sparkled like jewels.

Franny and Jeremy walked right through them. Their eyes didn't leave the mailbox.

The two boys and I stepped a little closer, eager to see better.

No sign of anyone inside the house.

We stepped even closer.

At last, Jeremy pulled down the metal mailbox lid. He and Franny raised their plastic jugs.

They both lowered the jugs to the mailbox.

And poured.

The water made a soft splashing sound as it hit the metal mailbox.

Franny emptied her jug. Jeremy had nearly emptied his.

Then the front door swung open—and Vanessa burst out. She wore a flowing, black dress. Her straight black hair flew wildly behind her.

Her black-lipsticked lips were open in an angry cry.

The cat screeched shrilly from somewhere in the house.

Franny dropped her jug. She bent to pick it up.

Changed her mind.

Ran.

Jeremy was already diving into the bushes at the far side of the house. Franny ran close behind him.

Cole, Anthony and I hadn't moved.

We stood in the grass. Frozen. Watching Vanessa.

I gasped when I saw Vanessa's furious stare.

I turned to Cole and Anthony. "Why is she staring like that at *us*?" I choked out. "Does she think *we* did it?"

My whole body stiffened. As if Vanessa's eyes were shooting out some kind of laser ray.

I forced myself to spin away. And I started to run.

Cole and Anthony were at my sides. Our trainers thudded heavily over the dirt path. We kicked up clouds of dirt as we ran. A blur of green and brown, the fields appeared to tilt and sway around me.

We ran through town without stopping. Without saying a word. Without even *looking* at each other!

Mrs Wagner stepped out of the bakery. She started to say hello. I caught the shocked expression on her face as the three of us ran past her without slowing down.

We ran until we reached my house. We burst through the gate, slamming it open so hard, the whole fence shook. I pushed open the front door with my shoulder, and all three of us staggered into the living room.

Gasping for breath, I dropped to my knees on the carpet.

Cole and Anthony collapsed on to the couch.

We struggled to catch our breath. I brushed my hair back off my sweaty forehead. The clock on the mantelpiece chimed. Three o'clock.

Cole and Anthony burst out laughing.

I narrowed my eyes at them. "What's so funny?" I demanded breathlessly.

That made them laugh even harder.

"What's so funny, guys?" I repeated. I climbed to my feet and pressed my hands into my waist, waiting for an answer. "Why are you laughing?"

"I don't know!" Cole answered finally.

"I don't know, either!" Anthony echoed.

And they both laughed again.

"You're crazy," I muttered, shaking my head. "That wasn't funny. It was scary."

Cole pulled himself up. His expression turned serious. "Did you see the way Vanessa stared at us?"

"She didn't see Franny and Jeremy," Anthony said. "She only saw us." He pulled off his glasses and cleaned them on his T-shirt sleeve. The short black hair on his round head glistened with sweat.

I felt a chill. "What if Vanessa decides to do something terrible to us?" I demanded. "You two won't be laughing then."

Cole pulled himself up even straighter. He ran

a hand back through his wavy blond hair. Cole is tall and even skinnier than me. Sometimes I think he looks like a grasshopper.

"Crystal, what do you mean?" he demanded softly.

"I mean, if Vanessa thinks *we* were the ones who filled her mailbox with water, maybe she'll pay *us* back. You know. Make our heads swell up or something."

"But we didn't do anything!" Anthony protested. "We have to tell her it was Franny and Jeremy."

"Snitch," Cole muttered, grinning at his friend.

"Maybe she won't give us a chance to explain," I said. "Maybe she'll just do something horrible to us."

I started to the kitchen. "You guys want something to drink?"

I didn't hear their replies.

I pulled open the fridge and took out a bottle of iced tea.

A second later, I opened my mouth in a loud scream of pain.

"Crystal—what happened?" Cole came running into the kitchen.

I shuddered in pain. "Ohhhh."

"What *happened?*" he cried.

I shook my hand, trying to shake away the throbbing. "The fridge door," I managed to choke out. "I—slammed it on my hand."

I shook my hand some more. Then I tested each finger. I could move them. Nothing broken.

I raised my eyes to Cole. "Why are you grinning?" I demanded.

"You didn't slam the door on your hand," he replied. "Vanessa did!"

Anthony giggled from the doorway.

"Cole—you're not funny!" I screeched. I wrapped my fingers around his scrawny neck and pretended to strangle him. But my hand still hurt. I had to let go.

"Vanessa cursed you," Anthony said, picking up where Cole had left off. "Now your hand will probably swell up to the size of a melon."

"And it will get soft and squishy like Tommy's head," Cole added gleefully. "Soft and squishy— like your *brain*!"

"Not funny! Not funny!" I insisted. I admit it. I felt a little afraid. I didn't like joking about this stuff.

My hand ached and burned. I opened the freezer and stuck it inside. "What if Vanessa really *has* powers?" I asked them. "What if she really did make me slam the door on my hand?"

Cole and Anthony raised their hands in front of them and began moving them back and forth, as if casting spells on me. "You are a *sponge head*!" Cole cried, lowering his voice, trying to sound like a real sorcerer. "You will mop up the dinner plates with your head!"

That's when Mum and Dad walked in.

"What on earth—?" Mum cried. "Crystal— why do you have your hand in the freezer?"

"Oh. Uh . . ." I slid my hand out and closed the freezer door. "Just cooling off," I said.

Mum narrowed her eyes at me. "Cooling off one hand?"

"Actually, I slammed a door on it," I told her.

"Vanessa slammed a door on it," Cole corrected.

"Vanessa?" Dad asked, crossing to the sink. "You mean that strange woman who lives outside of town?"

"Have you been pestering that poor woman again?" Mum demanded. "Don't you kids have anything better to do than sneak around and play tricks on her?"

"We didn't do anything," Cole said. "Really."

"That's the truth," Anthony chimed in.

"Then why did you mention Vanessa?" Mum asked Cole.

I decided I'd better change the subject. "Where were you two?" I asked my parents.

"Out the back. Trying to decide where to put the fence for the vegetable garden," Dad replied. He was washing his hands in the kitchen sink, something Mum always scolds him for.

"If we didn't have chickens, you wouldn't need a fence," I grumbled. "I think you should get rid—"

"That reminds me," Mum interrupted. "Cole, some of the chickens wandered all the way to the back. Would you go out and round them up, please?"

"Chicken Roundup!" I exclaimed gleefully. I slapped Cole on the back. "Congrats! Your favourite job!"

"But that's not fair! I did the chicken roundup last time!" Cole wailed. "It's Crystal's turn!"

"I fed them this morning," I declared. "And it wasn't even my turn. Besides, it's easier for you to round them up. Because you look like a big rooster!"

Everyone laughed except Cole. He grumbled and shook his head. Then he grabbed Anthony and pulled him outside to help with the chicken roundup.

A few seconds later, I could hear a lot of clucking and squawking back there. And I could hear the boys shouting and complaining.

Have you ever tried to herd chickens?

It isn't easy.

My hand ached all day from slamming it in the fridge door. And every time it ached, I thought of Vanessa.

And I pictured her cold eyes, staring at the boys and me.

She isn't going to do anything to us, I told myself. She *can't* do anything to us. Those stories about Vanessa can't be true.

I kept repeating this to myself. But that night, I had trouble falling asleep.

I kept seeing a shadow move against my bedroom wall. The shadow of a cat.

I climbed out of bed and pulled down the window blind. Now the room was bathed in total darkness. No shadows on the wall.

I still couldn't fall asleep.

I stared wide-eyed into the blackness.

"Crystal, go to sleep," I instructed myself. "You are scaring yourself for no reason."

A creaking sound made me jump.

A crack of grey light at my bedroom door.

Another creak—and the streak of light grew wider.

I swallowed hard.

I watched the door slowly slide open.

Staring in silence, I realized that someone was creeping into my bedroom.

Someone wearing a black veil. And a long black dress.

Vanessa!

I opened my mouth to scream. But only a low moan came out.

I started to jump out of bed. But where could I run?

She slid silently towards me, arms reaching out as if ready to grab me. Her face was hidden behind the heavy black veil.

How did she get in the house?

What is she going to do to me?

The frightening questions fluttered through my mind.

She leaned over my bed. Her hands moved to my throat.

"No!" I choked out.

I reached up. Pushed away her hands. Grasped her veil in both hands. And tugged it off.

Cole!

In the grey light from the open doorway, I could see his grin.

"Cole—you *jerk*!" I shrieked.

21

I tossed the veil down. Leapt for him. Tried to tackle him to the floor.

But I missed—and tumbled out of bed.

"Cole—you creep! You scared me to death!"

I don't think he heard me over his gleeful laughter.

I scrambled to my feet. He dodged away from me. Still cackling, he backed to the doorway. "You really thought it was Vanessa!" he cried.

"Did not!" I lied. "You just scared me, that's all."

"Did too!" he insisted. "You thought it was Vanessa. You really thought she had come to pay you back!"

"Did not! Did not!" I cried angrily.

He made hand motions as if casting a spell. "Abracadabra! You're a sponge head!"

He started laughing again. He really thought he was a riot.

"I'll pay you back!" I promised him. "Really. I'm going to pay you back!"

Shaking his head, he made his way out of the room, the long black skirt trailing over the floor. With an angry growl, I picked up the veil and heaved it after him.

I punched my pillow furiously. Why did I let him fool me like that? Now he'd tell everyone in school that I thought Vanessa was sneaking into my room.

My heart still pounding, I climbed back into

bed. I felt so angry, it took me hours to fall asleep. And when I finally drifted off, I dreamed about a cat.

An ugly black cat with bright yellow eyes and a blood-red tongue.

The cat hunched in an all-white room. But then the room became my room.

In the dream, the cat moved to the end of my bed. It opened its mouth wide. The bright red tongue darted over its yellow teeth.

And then the cat began to screech.

A sharp, painful sound—like fingernails dragged over a blackboard.

It screeched. And screeched. Its mouth opened wider. Its yellow eyes flamed.

I couldn't stand the sound. In the dream, I saw myself cover my ears with both hands.

But the shrill screeching grew even louder.

The cat floated closer. Closer. Opened its jaws wide, as if to swallow me.

I woke up, stunned by the sudden silence.

The dream had been so real. I expected to see the screeching cat standing on my bedcovers.

Bars of yellow sunlight fell through the window blinds on to my floor. I saw the crumpled black veil beside the door.

No cat.

I stretched and climbed out of bed. Yawning, I got dressed for school.

Mum was setting down a bowl of cornflakes

and a glass of orange juice for me when I reached the kitchen. "Sleep well?" she asked.

"Not at all," I grumbled. I dropped into my seat at the breakfast table. "First I couldn't get to sleep. Then I had an annoying nightmare."

Mum tsk-tsked. She crossed to the sink and began pouring water into the coffee-maker.

I thought about telling her about Cole's stupid joke. But I decided not to. Mum would only start asking us again about what we were doing at Vanessa's house yesterday.

"What are you doing after school, Crystal?" she asked, clicking on the coffeemaker. "Maybe you can come home and rest up then."

"No way," I replied, swallowing a mouthful of cornflakes. "I've got basketball practice. Coach Clay says she's going to give me extra playing time. I told her how tired I am of being the *sixth* girl. I want to be a starter. But I never get enough playing time to show how good I am."

Mum turned to me. She blew a strand of brown hair off her forehead. "Maybe that's why you couldn't sleep last night," she said. "Maybe you were nervous about basketball practice."

I shrugged. I didn't want to tell her the real reason.

I heard Cole clomping down the stairs. Mum pulled out a cereal bowl for him.

"When are you going to buy a birthday present

for Lucy-Ann?" Mum asked me. "You know her birthday party is Saturday."

Lucy-Ann is one of my best friends. She has been talking about this birthday—her thirteenth!—for weeks. She's so excited about becoming a teenager.

"Maybe I'll go shopping tomorrow after school," I replied.

"What are you going to get her?"

I opened my mouth to answer, but Cole came charging into the room.

One look at his face—and Mum and I both gasped.

"Cole!" Mum cried.

"My f-face . . ." he stammered.

His cheeks and forehead were covered with big sores. Ugly red blotches.

"It . . . hurts . . ." he groaned. He turned to me. "Vanessa," he murmured. "Vanessa did this to me."

Cole dropped to his knees and covered his face with his hands.

I jumped up from my chair. "Cole—?"

"I'll call the doctor!" Mum cried. "Or should I call an ambulance?" She bent over Cole. "Does it really hurt? Are you really in pain?"

Cole slowly lowered his hands. And as he did, I saw the broad grin on his face.

And I saw that his hands had smeared the red blotches on his cheeks.

"Cole!" I screamed furiously.

Mum's mouth dropped open. She had one hand on the phone, ready to call the doctor.

"Red marker pen," Cole said through his grin. Then he burst out laughing.

"Aaaagggh!" I let out a furious cry—and heaved my cereal spoon at him. It bounced off his chest and clattered across the linoleum floor.

"Not funny!" I screamed.

Mum shook her head. "Cole, you really scared me." She sighed.

Cole stood up and pointed at me. "Crystal, you really believed Vanessa did it to me," he accused.

"Your jokes are just stupid!" I cried. "I'm never going to believe you again. Even if you get hit by a truck, I won't believe you!"

I spun around and stormed out of the kitchen.

Behind me, I could hear Mum telling Cole, "You really have to stop scaring your sister."

"Why?" Cole asked.

I grabbed my backpack, tore out of the house, and slammed the door behind me.

I forced Vanessa from my mind.

I didn't think about her once that whole day.

In fact, I didn't think about her until the next time I saw her.

And that's when all the frightening stuff really started.

"Is that Lucy-Ann's cake?" Cole asked.

"Well, it says HAPPY BIRTHDAY, LUCY-ANN on it," I replied. "So what's *your* guess, genius?"

Cole, Anthony and I had our noses pressed against the window of the bakery. Several white-frosted birthday cakes were on display. Lucy-Ann's stood in the middle of the shelf, ready to be picked up for her party on Saturday.

I saw Mrs Wagner waving to us from behind the counter inside the shop. I waved back to her. Then I checked my watch.

"Hey—I'm late," I told the boys. "I've got to buy a present for Lucy-Ann. Then I've got to get home and study my maths."

I hurried towards the Mini-Mart on the corner next to the grocery. My plan was to buy Lucy-Ann a new CD. At the end of the block, Mr Horace's old hound sprawled in the middle of Main Street, lazily scratching his mangy ear with a back paw, looking as if he owned the town.

I heard Cole and Anthony laughing behind me. I turned and made a shooing motion with both hands: "Take a walk, guys. You don't have to tag along with me."

They ignored me, as usual.

Cole slipped an egg from his pocket. His eyes flashed mischievously. "Think fast!" he cried. He tossed the egg at Anthony.

Anthony cupped his hands and caught the egg. Without a pause, he tossed it back to my brother.

"Oh, please," I begged. "Not this stupid game."

Cole had to stretch—but he caught the egg in one hand.

This is one of their games that drives me crazy. They throw an egg back and forth, back and forth as they walk. Each time they throw it, they stand a little farther apart from each other. The idea is to see how far they can throw the egg without breaking it.

The answer usually is: not too far.

One of them always ends up with egg splattered all over him. Once I made the mistake of trying to dive between them and intercept the egg. Too bad I intercepted it with my *forehead*.

"Please, guys," I begged. "Go and do your egg-throwing somewhere else—okay?"

Cole backed into the middle of the street. A few metres away, Mr Horace's old hound yawned and rolled on to his back. I saw two men in overalls pulling enormous sacks of feed from the Feed Store across the street.

"Yo!" Cole called—and heaved the egg high in the air.

Anthony raised a hand to shield his eyes from the sun. He backed up, back, back—nearly to the grocery shop.

And the egg plopped down on top of his head.

What a disgusting *craaack* it made. Really gross.

"Huh?" Anthony uttered a startled gasp. And yellow goo started to flow down his forehead and the sides of his hair.

"Sorry. It got away from me!" Cole cried. But he couldn't keep a straight face. He burst out laughing.

Anthony let out an angry growl and charged at Cole.

Cole dodged away from him and ran up on to the pavement.

"Stop it! Stop it!" I shouted.

Roaring like an angry lion, Anthony leapt at my brother and pinned him against the grocer's window. "You did that on purpose!" he shouted.

"No way! It was an accident!" Cole replied, laughing.

Anthony lowered his egg-gloppy head and head-butted Cole in the chest.

"Ooof!" My brother let out a groan.

Anthony pulled back his head and prepared another head butt.

Cole glanced down at his T-shirt. It was drenched in sticky egg yolk.

"Stop it! Stop it!" Shrieking, I leapt between them. I grabbed Anthony's shoulders and tried to tug him off Cole.

I didn't see Vanessa step out of the grocer's. None of us did.

"Get *off*!" I begged Anthony. I gave him a hard tug.

And all three of us bounced hard into Vanessa. First I saw her black dress. Then I saw her pale face. Saw her dark eyes go wide with surprise.

I saw her mouth fall open. Her hands fly up.

And two bags of groceries bounced to the pavement.

I heard one bag rip. And I heard cans and bottles clatter on to the street.

The sound of shattering glass made me turn to the street. I saw a puddle of deep red ketchup spread from a broken ketchup bottle. A carton of eggs lay open and shattered in the gutter.

I still had Anthony's shoulders gripped in both hands. A shiver ran down his body. He pulled free of me with a hard jerk.

"Sorry!" he cried to Vanessa. "I'm really sorry!"

Then he jumped over some of her groceries— and went running into the street.

"Whooooa!" Anthony cried out as he tripped over the hound dog. He went down face first on the pavement on top of the dog.

The dog didn't make a sound. It hardly moved.

Anthony struggled to his feet. Then he roared off behind the Feed Store. He disappeared without ever looking back.

"Oh, wow," I murmured, staring down at the ruined groceries all over the street. "Oh, wow."

Cole stood beside me, breathing noisily, shaking his head.

The dog loped over slowly, favouring one leg. He lowered his head and began licking egg yolk off the pavement.

I turned to Vanessa and nearly gasped when I saw the look of fury on her cold, pale face.

As her eyes locked on mine, I felt as if I'd been stabbed—by an icicle.

A shiver of fear made me take a step back. I grabbed Cole's arm. I started to pull him away.

But Vanessa stepped forward, her long black dress sweeping along the pavement. She pointed to Cole with a slender finger tipped in black nail polish. Then she pointed at me.

"Chicken chicken," she whispered.

A smile spread over Vanessa's black-lipsticked lips as she rasped those words at us.

"Chicken chicken."

I gasped as if I'd been slapped.

The street tilted in front of me. Then it started to spin.

What on earth did she mean? Why did she say that?

Cole and I didn't wait to ask her. Our trainers thudded on the pavement as we took off, running at full speed.

I glimpsed the old hound dog, still lapping up egg yolk from the street. And I glimpsed Vanessa's angry face for one more brief second.

And then Cole and I whipped around the corner, sped past the post office and the dry cleaner, and ran all the way home.

I didn't glance back once. And I didn't say a word until we were safely in the kitchen.

I collapsed on to a kitchen stool. Cole ran the

cold water in the sink and splashed it over his face and hair.

We were both panting and wheezing, too breathless to speak. I wiped the sweat off my forehead with my arm. Then I crossed to the fridge and pulled out a small bottle of water. Twisting off the cap, I tilted it to my mouth and drank it down.

"We should have stayed," I finally managed to sputter.

"Huh?" Cole turned to me. He had water dripping down his red face. The front of his T-shirt was soaked.

"We should have stayed and helped Vanessa pick up her groceries," I told him.

"No way!" Cole protested. "She's crazy! Did you see the look on her face?"

"Well . . . we knocked down all of her groceries," I said.

"So? It was an accident," my brother insisted. "Accidents happen all the time, right? But she . . . she wanted to *destroy* us!"

I rubbed the cool bottle against my pounding forehead. "Why did she say that to us?" I asked, thinking out loud. "Why did she whisper like that?"

Cole changed his expression. He reached out his hand and pointed a finger at me. Then he did a pretty good Vanessa imitation. "Chicken chicken!" he rasped, shaking his finger at me.

"Stop it!" I snapped. "I mean, really. Stop it, Cole. You're giving me the creeps."

"Chicken chicken," he whispered again.

"Come on. Give me a break," I pleaded. I crushed the plastic bottle in my hand. "It's just so weird," I murmured. "Why did she say that word? Why?"

Cole shrugged. "Because she's crazy?"

I shook my head fretfully. "She isn't crazy. She's evil," I said. I wrapped my arms around myself. "I just have this feeling that something horrible is going to happen now."

Cole rolled his eyes. "Crystal—what could happen?"

"Did you buy a present for Lucy-Ann?" Mum asked at dinner.

I swallowed a forkful of spaghetti. "Well . . . actually . . . no."

She gazed up at me in surprise. "But I thought you went into town to buy her a CD."

"Pass the Parmesan cheese," Dad interrupted. So far, those were his only words this evening. Guess he had a bad day at work.

"I don't understand," Mum insisted. "What did you do after school, Crystal?"

"Nothing, Mum." I sighed. "Can we change the subject?"

"You have spaghetti sauce all over your chin," Cole pointed out.

I made a face at him. "Very helpful," I muttered. "Guess I've been sitting across the table from *you* for too long. I'm picking up your habits."

He stuck out his tongue at me. He had half a meatball on his tongue. Very mature.

"I forgot to ask you about basketball practice yesterday," Dad chimed in. "How did that—"

"Bad subject!" I interrupted.

Mum set down her fork. She blew a strand of hair off her forehead. "Guess every subject is a bad one tonight, huh?"

"Maybe," I grumbled, lowering my eyes to my plate. I shook my head. "I was terrible at practice. Coach Clay gave me a chance, and I played like a total no-hoper."

"No one's perfect," Cole chimed in.

"Cole, be quiet," Mum scolded.

"Doesn't anyone want to hear about my sprained thumb?" Cole whined.

"No," Mum shot back. "Be quiet." She turned back to me. "You didn't play well?"

"I—I tripped over my own dribble. Twice," I stammered. "And I missed an easy layup. The ball didn't even touch the rim."

"Well . . . next time . . ." Dad started.

"But this was my big chance to show I can be a starter!" I cried. "And I blew it. I just felt so tired. I hadn't slept the night before. And . . . and . . ."

"You're still the sixth player," Mum said soothingly. "You'll get a chance."

"Do you have team practice tomorrow?" Dad asked, helping himself to more salad.

I shook my head. "No. Tomorrow afternoon is chorus practice. Cole has it, too. You know. The chorus is performing for the junior high graduation next month."

"I get to sing two solos," Cole bragged. "I'm the only fifth grader in the chorus—and I'm the only one with perfect pitch."

"No one's perfect," I reminded him. I know. It was a really lame joke. No one laughed.

Mum lowered her eyes to Cole's hand. "How did you sprain your thumb?" she asked.

"I didn't," Cole replied. "I was just trying to get into the conversation."

Mrs Mellon, the music teacher, was a tiny, birdlike woman. She always wore grey sweaters and grey skirts or trousers. With her feathery grey hair and snipped beak of a nose, she always reminded me of a sparrow. Or maybe a chirping budgie.

She called us her canaries.

Greene County Middle School wasn't big enough to have a music room. So the chorus met after school in a corner of the auditorium stage.

There were eight kids in the chorus. Four boys and four girls. Mostly sixth graders, with a few younger kids like Cole thrown in. It was hard to put a chorus together in such a small school.

Mrs Mellon was late. So the boys shot paper clips across the stage at each other with rubber bands. And the girls talked about how dumb the boys were.

When Mrs Mellon finally arrived, her hands fluttering tensely at her feathery hair, she wanted to get right down to business. "Our performance is two weeks from tonight," she announced fretfully. "And we really don't know what we're doing—do we?"

We all pretty much agreed that we needed a lot more rehearsal time. Lucy-Ann, who is our only soprano, raised her hand. "Maybe we could lipsynch some songs," she suggested. "You know. From records."

Everyone laughed.

I studied Lucy-Ann. I wasn't so sure she was joking.

"No fooling around this afternoon," Mrs Mellon said sternly. "Let's see how much we can get done when we're being serious."

We sang our warm-up scales. We were interrupted when a large black spider dropped from the rafters into Lucy-Ann's curly, blonde hair. She shrieked and staggered back. And she began shaking her head wildly and tugging at her curls with both hands.

Finally, the spider dropped on to the stage floor, and Cole stamped on it.

"Isn't that bad luck or something?" a boy named Larry called to my brother.

Cole shrugged and scraped his shoe against the floor.

"Let's begin with 'Beautiful Ohio'," Mrs

Mellon suggested, ignoring the whole spider problem. She shuffled sheet music on her music stand. "That's the one that gave us so much trouble last time."

"It's the high part that's the problem," Lucy-Ann chimed in.

"It's your *voice* that's the problem!" Larry teased Lucy-Ann. I think he has a crush on her. He's always insulting her.

Mrs Mellon cleared her throat. "Please, folks. Serious. Serious." She turned to Cole. "Have you been practising your solo?"

"Oh, yeah. Sure," my brother lied.

"Then let's try it," Mrs Mellon suggested. "Remember, Cole—you wait *three* beats before you come in."

"No problem," Cole told her.

At the last rehearsal, he didn't do it right *once*.

Mrs Mellon raised her arms. Smiled. And fluttered her hands, her signal for us to start.

We began to sing "Beautiful Ohio". It's kind of a drippy song, but I like to sing the high part.

"Very good. Very good," Mrs Mellon encouraged us as we sang, a tight smile on her face.

It *did* sound pretty good.

Until Cole began his solo.

I saw him take a deep breath. He stepped forward. Waited for three beats. Opened his mouth.

And sang: "BLUCK BUCK BUCK BLU-UUCK BLUCK."

"Huh?" Mrs Mellon gasped.

We all stopped singing. I stared hard at my brother.

He had a confused expression on his face. He kept clearing his throat.

"Sing the words, Cole," Mrs Mellon instructed sternly. "You *do* know the words—right?"

Cole nodded.

"Let's begin with the chorus just before Cole's solo," she told us.

We began again. As I sang, I kept my eyes on my brother.

I saw him count off the three beats. Then:

"BLUCK BLUCK BLUCK CLUCK BUCK!"

What was he trying to prove?

Larry laughed. But no one else did.

Cole kept rubbing his neck and clearing his throat. His face was bright red.

"*Are you okay?*" I mouthed the words to him.

He didn't answer me.

"Cole—please!" Mrs Mellon pleaded. "Stop fooling around. We really haven't time." She frowned at him. "You have a beautiful voice. I know you can sing this. Will you please do your part?"

She raised her hands. "Begin on three," she

told him. "One . . . two . . . three . . ." She began conducting with one hand. "Now let's hear your best," she urged.

"BLUCK BLUCK BUCK BUCK BUCK!" my brother clucked in a high, silly voice.

I stepped away from the other girls and rushed up to him. "Cole—what is the big idea?" I cried furiously. "Why are you doing that?"

"BLUCK BLUCK BUCK CLUCK BLUCK," he replied.

Later, I was up in my room, wrapping Lucy-Ann's birthday present. I glanced to the doorway and saw Cole standing there tensely.

His blond hair stood up straight on top of his head. He was wiping his sweaty hands on the front of his T-shirt.

"What do you want?" I asked sharply. "I'm busy." I folded a corner of the birthday wrapping paper and taped it down over the CD case.

Cole cleared his throat, but didn't reply.

I shook my head at him. "You ruined the whole rehearsal," I told him.

"It wasn't my fault!" he cried shrilly.

"Hah!" I slammed my scissors down on the desk. "You refused to sing. You stood there clucking like a hen! Whose fault *was* it?"

"You don't understand—" Cole croaked, tenderly rubbing his throat.

"No, I don't," I interrupted angrily. "You know, we're all tired of your stupid jokes.

Especially me. You just think you're so funny all the time, Cole. But you're really such a pain."

"But I wasn't being funny!" he protested, stepping into the room. He walked up to the desk and fiddled nervously with the tape dispenser. "I didn't want to cluck like that. I—I couldn't help it."

I rolled my eyes. "For sure," I muttered.

"No—really, Crystal. I—I think Vanessa made me do it! I think she made me cluck like that!"

I laughed. "I'm not stupid, you know," I told him. "I may fall for the same joke of yours once or twice. But I'm not going to fall for it again."

"But Crystal—"

"It wasn't funny," I repeated. "And it wasn't fair for you to ruin the whole rehearsal for everyone."

"You don't understand!" Cole protested. "It wasn't a joke. I really *had* to cluck. I—"

"Out!" I shouted. I made shooing motions with both hands. "Out of my room—now!"

His face turned bright red. He started to say something. Changed his mind with a defeated sigh. Turned and slumped out of my room.

"Anything for a joke, huh, Cole?" I murmured to myself.

I'm usually not that mean to my brother. But this time he deserved to be taught a lesson.

I finished wrapping the present. Then I did homework until bedtime.

I turned out the light and was climbing between the sheets when I heard a chicken clucking.

That's weird, I thought. I never hear the chickens at night. They're all locked in their coop.

"*Cluuuuck bluuuuuuck.*"

Sitting up, I stared across the dark room to the open window. My curtains fluttered in a soft breeze. A triangle of pale moonlight slanted over the carpet.

Had the chicken coop door come open? I wondered.

Had a chicken escaped somehow?

"*Bluuck bluuck buuck.*"

The cry seemed to be coming from close to the house, beneath my bedroom window.

Watching the fluttering curtains, I climbed out of bed and crossed the room to the window. The moonlight washed over me, cold and silvery.

"*Bluck bluck cluck.*"

I leaned on the window ledge. Peered down to the ground.

And gasped.

Nothing down there.

No chicken.

I stared at the silvery ground. Then moved my eyes to the long chicken coop beside the garage. It sort of looked like a long, low, wooden doghouse. The door was shut tight. Nothing moved inside its tiny round windows.

"*Bluuuuck bluuuck.*"

Feeling confused, I pulled my head inside. Where was that clucking coming from?

From inside?

"*Cluuck cluuuck.*"

Yes. I could hear it through the wall. The wall to my brother's room next door.

Why is he doing that? I asked myself, climbing back into bed. Why is he in there clucking in the middle of the night?

What is he trying to prove?

I knew Lucy-Ann's birthday party would be fun. Lucy-Ann always throws great parties.

She comes from a big farm family. She has seven brothers and sisters.

Their big farmhouse is always filled with great smells—chickens roasting, pies baking. Lucy-Ann's parents are the most successful farmers in Goshen Falls. And they're really nice people, too.

Lucy-Ann invited the whole class to her party, and about two dozen of her relatives. It was a beautiful spring afternoon. And a lot of people were already out in the yard in front of the tall, white farmhouse when I arrived.

Lucy-Ann has a lot of little cousins. As I hurried up the gravel drive, I saw a group of them hanging around the side of the utility barn. Lucy-Ann's dad was giving tractor rides, and the little kids were jumping up and down, wrestling each other in excitement, waiting their turns.

I met Lucy-Ann at the top of the drive and handed her the wrapped-up CD.

She studied the square-shaped box and grinned. "Wow. I'll *never* guess what this is!" she joked.

"Okay, okay. So I'm not very original," I replied with a shrug.

"You don't know what a perfect present it is," she said as we began to walk across the grass to the others. "Mum and Dad got me a Discman for my birthday—but no CDs."

I laughed. "Well, now you've got *one*," I said.

"At least I know you don't already have it!"

Lucy-Ann's expression turned serious. "Are you going to chorus rehearsal tomorrow morning?"

I nodded. "Yeah. We really need to practise."

"I'll be a little late," Lucy-Ann said. "We usually don't get back from church till after eleven-thirty." She frowned. "Did you talk to your brother? Why did he act like such a total jerk yesterday? What was all that horrible clucking? Did he think it was funny or something?"

I shrugged. "Yeah. I guess." Then I added with a sigh, "No way I can explain my brother. Sometimes I think he's from Mars."

Lucy-Ann laughed. "Tell me about it," she muttered. "I've got *four* brothers!"

I waved to a couple of girls from my class who were leaning against the broad trunk of an old maple tree. I walked over to talk to them.

I like a lot of kids in my class, although I don't get to see some of them outside of school. You see, Goshen Falls is so tiny, and we have the only middle school for miles. So kids are bussed to our school from all over the county.

That means some of my friends live over thirty miles away. When I want to call them at night, it's a long-distance call!

It was a nice party. We stayed outside the whole time. Lucy-Ann cranked up the volume on her tape player, and we all danced. I mean,

48

all the girls danced. A couple of the boys joined in. But most of them stood on the grass, making jokes about those who were dancing.

I really had fun—until birthday cake time.

And then the fun turned to horror.

As the afternoon sun started to lower itself behind the farmhouse, Lucy-Ann's mum carried out the birthday cake. Actually, she carried out *two* cakes—one vanilla from the bakery and one chocolate that she'd baked herself.

"With so many kids in our family," Lucy-Ann explained to me, "no one could ever decide what kind of cake everyone liked best. So Mum always has to bake an extra one for every birthday!"

We all grabbed plates and gathered around the long, white-tableclothed table to sing "Happy Birthday" to Lucy-Ann. Beside the two cakes stood a blueberry pie about the size of a pizza!

It took a long while to light the candles on both cakes. The wind kept gusting and blowing some of the candles out.

Finally, Lucy-Ann's parents got them all lit, and we sang "Happy Birthday". Lucy-Ann looked really pretty standing behind the cakes, the flickering candlelight dancing over her face and curly blonde hair.

She seemed to be staring at me as we sang.

And I suddenly realized that something was wrong.

That loud clicking sound I heard—it was coming from me!

My lips were clicking together noisily as I sang.

As soon as the song ended, I rubbed my lips with my finger. They felt very dry. Sort of cracked and dry.

"Crystal—what kind of cake?" Lucy-Ann was asking. I gazed up to see her and her mother slicing the cakes.

I held my plate up. "A little bit of both?" I couldn't decide, either.

Balancing my plate and fork in one hand, I walked off to join some friends. "Looks good," I said.

I mean, I tried to say it. But it came out, "*Tcccck tccccck*." Sort of a metal click.

I ran my tongue over my lips. So dry.

"*Tcccck tccccccck*."

I tried to chew a forkful of cake. But each bite made that loud clicking sound.

I licked my lips again.

Tried to chew.

I started to choke. I couldn't chew the cake.

"*Ckkkkkkk tccccck*."

A few kids were staring at me.

"Crystal, are you okay?" someone asked.

I clicked a reply. Then I hurried to Lucy-Ann at the table. "Do you have any Chap Stick?" I demanded shrilly.

My lips clicked as I talked. She struggled to understand me.

"Chap Stick?" I repeated. *"Chpsttttccck?"*

She nodded, narrowing her eyes to study me. "In the medicine chest. Downstairs bathroom on the left." She pointed.

I set down my cake plate and took off, running across the grass. I pulled open the screen door and flew into the house. It smelled sweet inside, from all the cake and pie baking.

I turned to the left, into the hallway. I knew my way. I'd spent a lot of hours with Lucy-Ann here.

The bathroom door stood open. I stepped inside, clicked on the light, and shut the door behind me.

Then I leapt to the medicine cabinet and gazed into the mirror.

It took my eyes a few seconds to adjust. But when I could finally focus on my lips—I opened my mouth in a shrill scream of horror.

Bright red, my lips poked out from my face.

I ran a finger across them. Both lips were bumpy. Hard and bumpy.

I tapped my lips with my finger. It made a soft *click*.

My lips were *hard*. They didn't feel like skin any more! They felt as hard as fingernails!

"*Tcccck tcccck*."

I clicked them. Opened and closed my mouth. Staring hard at the ugly reflection in the mirror.

Had my lips grown some sort of crust? Were my real lips underneath?

I raised both hands and struggled to pull the crusty part off.

But no. No crust. The hard lips were attached to my face.

"Oww!" I gasped. My lips clicked shut.

"What is *happening* to me? It—it's like a *bird* beak! I can't let anyone see me like this!" I cried out loud.

I banged the mirror with both fists. This *can't* be happening! I told myself in a complete panic. It *can't*!

I tried to pull the hard beak lips off one more time.

"Crystal—calm down. Calm down!" I instructed myself. I took a deep breath and forced myself to turn away from the mirror.

It's an allergic reaction, I decided.

That's all. I ate something I am allergic to.

It will disappear in a few hours. And if it doesn't disappear, Dr Macy will know how to shrink the lips back to normal and make them soft again.

I took another deep breath. My whole body was shaking. I was trembling so hard, my lips were clicking.

I shut my eyes. Then I turned back to the mirror. I opened them, praying my real lips would be back.

But no.

"A bird beak," I murmured in a shaky whisper. "It looks like a bird beak."

Click click.

I ran my tongue over the bumpy lips.

Ow. The hard lips scratched my tongue.

I can't let anyone see me like this! I decided. I'll sneak out the front door and run home. I'll explain to Lucy-Ann later.

I shut off the light and pulled the bathroom

door open a crack. The house was empty. Every-one was still out in the back, enjoying the cakes and pie.

Will I ever enjoy cake again? I wondered.

Or will I have to pull up worms from the ground and suck them through my bird lips?

Sickening thoughts.

I crept along the living room. Then pushed open the front door—and escaped.

As I ran to the road, I could hear the happy voices from behind the house. Kids were laughing and shouting over the boom of dance music.

I turned and started running home at full speed. I hoped no one could see me.

The sun had sunk behind the trees. Evening shadows reached across the ground towards me.

My lips clicked as I ran. My heart pounded. I ran all the way home without slowing down once. Luckily, I didn't run into anyone I knew on the street.

Mum and Dad's car was gone. I ran up the driveway and into the house through the kitchen door.

Cole turned shakily from the sink. "Crystal—!" he cried. I could tell instantly that something was wrong.

I turned my face away. I didn't want him to see my ugly bird mouth.

But he rushed forward, grabbed my arm, and turned me around. "Mum and Dad aren't home," he murmured. "I—I have to show you something."

"Cole—what is it?" I demanded, my lips clicking. "Why are you—*click click*—wearing that bath towel around your neck?"

"I . . . need help," he replied, lowering his eyes.

He slowly unwrapped the blue bath towel. Then he slid it off his neck. "Look," he insisted.

I gasped.

Feathers!

He had white feathers poking out from his neck and shoulders.

"Cole—when did this happen?" I shrieked.

"*Bluccck bluuuck bucccck*," he clucked, his eyes wide with horror.

"Stop it!" I cried angrily. "This is no time for your stupid clucking!"

And then I realized that he had tricked me again. The feathers weren't really growing from his body. He had glued them on or something.

"*Bluuuck*. I . . . can't . . . stop the clucking!" he choked out, rubbing his throat.

"Yeah. Sure," I replied, rolling my eyes. I reached out and plucked a white feather from the back of his neck.

I expected the fake feather to slide off easily.

But my brother's hands shot up. "OUCH!" he screamed.

The tip of the feather left a small hole in his skin. I grabbed a big feather on his shoulder— and pulled it.

"Hey—careful!" Cole cried, moving away from

me. "*Bluuuck cluuuck*. That really hurts!"

"Oh, no!" I gasped. "They're real! You ... you're really growing—*click click*—feathers!"

"Uh ... uh ... uh ..." Cole started to whimper. His feathery shoulders shook up and down.

"Take it easy," I told him. I guided him gently into his room. "I'll pull them off. I'll be really careful. You'll be okay."

I made him sit down on the edge of the bed. I leaned over him and started to pluck out the white feathers. I tried to be as gentle as I could. But he jumped each time I tugged one out.

"We've got to tell Mum and Dad," he said softly, his eyes lowered to the floor. "Ouch."

"They're almost all out," I told him. I plucked a long one off the back of his neck. He jumped. "No problem. You will look perfectly normal."

"But we've still got to tell Mum and Dad," he insisted.

"Do you think they'll believe us?" I asked. My hard lips clicked with each word.

Cole gazed up at me. "Hey—what's up with your lips?"

"Oh—I—uh ..." I covered them with one hand. "Just chapped," I said. "Very chapped."

I don't know why. I didn't want to let him know that weird things were happening to me, too.

"You look disgusting!" Cole exclaimed. "Yuck!" It seemed to cheer him up a lot.

I tugged the last two feathers out as hard as I could.

"Hey—!" he cried out angrily. He rubbed a hand over the back of his neck.

I stepped back. White feathers covered the bed and floor. "You'd better pick them up," I clicked.

He clucked in reply.

I still had one hand over my mouth. I didn't need any more comments from him about how disgusting my lips looked. I hurried to the bathroom to find some cream for them.

Mum and Dad stayed out very late. Cole and I tried to stay awake because we wanted to talk to them. But finally, we gave up and went to bed.

Sunday morning I woke up late. The sun was already high in the sky. Orange sunlight washed over my room from the open window. A soft breeze ruffled my feathers.

Huh? Feathers?

"Ohhhh." I sat up with a groan. My neck itched like crazy. My arms itched, too.

I blinked myself awake. And stared at the white feathers up and down my arms.

I opened my mouth to scream. But all that came out was a choked "*goggle goggle goggle*". Like a clucking hen.

I leapt out of bed and hurtled to the dresser

mirror. I pulled down the top of my nightshirt and gasped. My shoulders and arms were covered with fluffy, white and brown feathers.

I brushed my hand over my lips. They had grown even harder. Hard as bone.

I saw something move in the mirror. I twirled around to find Cole in my bedroom doorway.

"Crystal—" he clucked. He staggered into the room. White feathers bristled on his shoulders and under his chin. They had grown back.

"Look at me!" I clicked.

"Blucck bluccck," Cole replied.

I turned back to the mirror and started frantically pulling off my feathers. It hurt each time. But I didn't care. I wanted them *off*!

It didn't take long. I plucked them all off. Then I gathered them up and tossed them into the wastebasket. Then I helped Cole remove his feathers.

His lips had hardened during the night. His fingernails had grown. His hands suddenly looked sort of like claws.

"Vanessa," he murmured.

I stared at him. I knew instantly what he meant.

I had been thinking the same thing all along. Remembering the horrible moment we spilled Vanessa's groceries.

"Yes," I agreed. "I didn't want to admit it. I didn't want to believe it. But Vanessa did this

60

to us. Vanessa is *bluuuucck bluccck* turning us into chickens."

"Chicken chicken," he clucked.

I heard clattering sounds downstairs in the kitchen. Mum and Dad!

"We have to *bluuuuck* tell them!" I cried. "We have to tell them everything!"

Cole and I both bolted for the bedroom door at the same time. We squeezed through together. Then we ran side by side down the hall.

I could hear Mum's voice from the kitchen.

Cole and I started calling to her as we hurried down the stairs.

"Mum—we need *bluuuucck* help!" I cried. "It's Vanessa. She really *does* have *bluuuucck cluuck* powers!"

"She's turning us into chickens!" Cole called to Mum as we reached the downstairs hall and went running to the kitchen. "We're growing feathers and everything!"

"It's the truth!" I cried. "You've got to help us. Cole and I—*bluuuck*—we're both turning into chickens!"

"That's good news," Mum replied calmly. "I need two more chickens for the barbecue this afternoon."

61

"Huh?"

"Barbecue us?"

Cole and I both gasped. Was Mum joking?

As soon as we burst into the kitchen, I realized that Mum wasn't talking to us. She was on the phone. She had her back to us and was drumming her fingernails on the Formica counter beside the phone.

My eyes swept over the kitchen. It was cluttered with pans and serving bowls, cut-up lettuce and tomatoes, a bag of potatoes, bottles of barbecue sauce and a pile of chicken parts on a tray beside the sink.

What a mess!

"Mum—we ... we *cluuuck bluuuck* have to talk to you!" I sputtered.

She turned, still talking, and waved. She said a few more words, then hung up the phone. "You two slept so late," she said, frowning at the wall clock. "It's nearly noon, and our guests will be here in an hour or two."

62

"Mum—" I started.

She wiped her forehead with the back of her hand and moved towards the sink. "Did you forget we're having a big barbecue this afternoon? We're having at least twenty guests, and—and—" She gestured to the pile of chicken parts.

The sight of them made my stomach turn.

"*Cluuucck bluuuck*," Cole murmured.

I stepped over to the sink. "We have to talk to you," I said, taking Mum's arm. "Cole and I—we have a problem. A real problem."

"About the chorus practice you missed this morning?" Mum interrupted. She took a small brush and began slapping barbecue sauce on the chicken parts. Then she tossed each part in a big china bowl.

"No, Mum. I—"

"That was Mrs Mellon on the phone," Mum continued. "She wondered where you were. She was calling to make sure you two were okay."

"We're *not* okay," I said solemnly.

"She's such a nice woman. She's bringing two barbecued chickens of her own this afternoon. For people who don't like them hot and spicy the way I make them."

She turned to me. "Crystal, you can help me cut up the peppers."

"Mum—please!" Cole cried. "Stop talking about the chickens!"

"We have something to tell you," I said.

"Your dad is out the back, getting the barbecue grilles ready," Mum said, brushing red sauce on a wing. "Oh! Ice! We have to remember to buy ice!"

"Mum—Cole and I are turning into chickens," I told her.

She laughed. "Ice and paper plates," she murmured. "I don't want to use real plates. Too much of a mess."

"No. Really!" I grabbed her arm. The brush fell into the chicken bowl.

"Crystal—I really don't have time," Mum sighed. She blew a strand of hair off her forehead and picked up the brush. "You and Cole should get yourself some breakfast—or lunch. Then see if you can help your dad."

"*Bluuuuck!*" Cole exclaimed.

"Listen to me, Mum," I begged. "Do you hear Cole clucking like that?"

"Yes. Very nice clucking," she murmured, tossing a chicken leg into the bowl.

"Do you see my lips?" I demanded. "Vanessa is doing this to us. We bumped Vanessa and spilled her groceries. So she is turning us *cluuuuck* into chickens."

"Please, you two," Mum groaned. "Can't you see how frantic I am? I don't have time to—"

She stopped when she glimpsed my lips. "Yuck! Those are really chapped."

64

"They're not chapped!" I screamed[...] ing a beak!"

"*Cluuuck bluuuck*," Cole added. [...]

Mum threw up her hands. "Go a[...] cream on your lips, Crystal. And ke[...] way, okay? I don't have time for jokes today. If you're not going to help, just don't make more trouble."

I turned to Cole. He shook his head unhappily.

We both slumped out of the room. "Do you think Dad will listen to us?" Cole asked weakly.

I clicked my lips. "I don't think so," I muttered. "He's as busy as Mum is."

"Then what can we do?" Cole asked. He scratched his neck. Were the feathers growing back already?

An idea popped into my head. "Anthony!" I cried.

"Huh? What about him?" Cole demanded.

"Anthony was with us!" I explained. "The same thing is probably happening to him. He's probably changing into a chicken like us."

Cole rubbed his chin hard. "*Cluuuuck. Bluuuuck*. Yeah. Probably."

"So if *all three* of us tell our story to Mum and Dad, then maybe they'll believe us!" I cried.

"It's worth a try," Cole agreed excitedly. "Let's hurry over to Anthony's house."

We each grabbed a glass of orange juice. And a Pop-Tart, which we ate raw.

hen we ran out the front door and headed to
Anthony's house.

We had run less than a block when we
bumped into Vanessa.

Well. This time we didn't really bump into her.

I saw her before Cole did, hurrying towards us on the other side of the street. Despite the heat, she was dressed all in black. She wore a black cotton shawl over the shoulders of her black dress. It fluttered behind her as she strode along.

"Oh—it's *her*!" Cole whispered, poking me in the side.

We both stopped in the middle of the pavement and stared open-mouthed as she approached.

Would she say something to us?

Could I work up the nerve to say something to her?

My heart pounded. My lips clicked nervously.

Cole's head started bobbing up and down on his neck. Just like a chicken. He let out a frightened cluck.

My poor brother.

Seeing him like that made me forget my fear. "Vanessa—!" I shouted.

She kept walking, taking those long, gliding strides of hers. Her shawl fluttered behind her.

"Vanessa—!" I repeated her name.

She had a look of solemn concentration on her face. I don't think she had even seen Cole and me.

Finally, she stopped. She stared across the street at us as if she didn't recognize us.

"*Bluuuuck bluuuck!*" my brother clucked angrily.

That brought a smile to her black-lipsticked lips. She laughed, and her dark eyes flashed.

She brushed back her straight, black hair. "Bluck bluck to you, too!" she called. "Chicken chicken!" Then she turned and hurried along the street.

"*Bluuuck*—wait!" Cole called after her. His head bobbed frantically up and down.

"You have to *help* us!" I cried, my hard lips clicking.

Vanessa began walking faster. Her black hair flew behind her. She didn't look back.

We found Anthony fiddling around with a golf club in his front yard. He had borrowed one of his dad's putters. And he had scooped out a hole in the middle of the grass.

We watched him sink a long putt as we ran across the front lawn. He flashed us two thumbs up. "Awesome, huh? I've been practising."

"Awesome," I muttered. I was still thinking about Vanessa, still feeling really upset and frightened.

"*Bluuck buuck,*" Cole said.

Anthony narrowed his eyes at him. "What's up, guys? My parents are going to your barbecue. But I have soccer practice."

Anthony pulled the ball from the hole and carried it a few metres away. He set it down, then leaned over the putter and prepared to putt again.

"Anthony, has anything weird been happening to you?" I blurted out.

"Yeah," Cole chimed in. "In the last two days—anything really weird?"

Anthony swung the golf club. It made a solid *thwock* as the club hit the ball. The ball sailed across the grass and stopped a few centimetres from the hole.

Anthony raised his eyes to us. "Yeah," he replied. "Something weird *has* been happening. How did you know?"

"Because *bluuuck* the same weird thing has been happening to us," I told him.

He stared hard at me. "Huh?"

Cole and I nodded.

Anthony made a face. He pretended to study

his golf club. "You mean you suddenly started putting really well, too?" he asked.

It was our turn to be surprised. "Putting? What does putting have to do with it?" I cried.

"Well, that's what's so weird," Anthony replied. "Before this weekend, I was a lousy putter. Really bad. I couldn't even play minigolf!"

"So what?" Cole chimed in.

"So this weekend I'm really good at it," Anthony continued. He twirled the club in his hand. "All of a sudden, I'm not a bad putter. Don't you think that's weird?"

"But—but—but—" I sputtered.

"What about growing feathers?" Cole demanded. "And what about your lips?"

Anthony's face filled with confusion. Then he turned to me. "What's with your brother? Is he going totally mental or what?"

"Are you clucking all the time?" Cole asked Anthony.

Anthony laughed. He cut it short quickly. "I don't get it. Is this a joke or something, guys?"

I pulled my brother to the driveway. "He doesn't know what we're talking about," I whispered. "For some reason, it isn't happening to him."

Cole's head bobbed up and down. He let out a low cluck.

"Let's go," I said. "Anthony isn't going to be any help."

"I don't get the joke," Anthony repeated.

"See you *bluuuck* later!" I called to him. I started pulling Cole down the street. "We've got to help out with the barbecue."

"Maybe I can come after soccer practice," Anthony called. "Save me some chicken!"

"Yeah. Sure," I muttered unhappily.

Guests were already arriving for the barbecue. I recognized my aunt Norma's red Honda in the driveway. And I saw the Walker family from down the block, heading around the side of the house to the back.

I ducked in through the front door and ran up to my room. I wanted to tell Mum what was happening to Cole and me. But I knew she was too busy. She wouldn't listen.

I closed the bedroom door carefully behind me. I didn't want anyone to see me until I'd checked myself out.

Sure enough, I found white and brown feathers sticking out from my neck and shoulders.

The feathers had just poked through the skin. So it was really hard to pull them out. I had to use tweezers for the smaller ones.

Pluck.

Pluck.

Pluck . . .

Ow. Did that hurt!

I heard voices from down in the backyard. And through my bedroom window, I could see swirling smoke from the barbecue grilles.

Ugh. I had always loved the aroma of barbecuing chicken. But now it sickened me. I felt my stomach lurch. I gagged. I held my hand over my mouth—my beak!—and waited for the nausea to fade.

I'll stay up in my room, I decided. I won't go downstairs.

But then I heard Mum calling me from the kitchen.

"Coming!" I yelled. I had no choice. I had to go down there.

I crossed my fingers on both hands. My fingers suddenly felt so bony, so scraggly. My nails were long and pointed. Maybe no one will notice what is happening to me, I prayed.

I made my way slowly downstairs to the kitchen. Mum had her hair tied up in a bun. She wore a long white apron, covered with barbecue sauce stains.

She was mixing a big bowl of salad. But she stopped when I slipped into the room. "Crystal, where have you been? Guests are arriving. I need you to go out and be a hostess while I finish up in here."

"Okay, Mum. No problem," I replied. I let out a couple of soft clucks.

"See if there is enough ice," Mum instructed. "And tell your dad he may need more charcoal. We—"

She stopped suddenly, with a gasp.

She stared out the window. "Crystal—what on earth is your brother doing out there?"

I stepped up beside her and gazed out the window. "Oh, no!" I cried.

I couldn't *believe* what I saw.

Cole had climbed into the area fenced off for the chickens. He was down on his elbows and knees. There were chickens all around him.

"What is he *doing*?" Mum repeated, raising a hand to one cheek.

I knew what he was doing. But I knew this wasn't the time to tell Mum. Not with twenty guests waiting for their dinner.

I peered out the window. Cole was pecking seeds off the ground.

I watched him lower his head to the gravel. I watched his lips open and his tongue slide out. I watched him suck up some chicken feed. His head bobbed up as he swallowed it down.

"Why is your brother being so stupid in front of company?" Mum asked, shaking her head. "Does he think that's *funny*?"

"I don't know, Mum," I replied. Cole's head lowered, and he sucked up more seed from the gravel.

People were laughing at him. Some just stared in confusion.

"Well, go out there and stop him," Mum ordered, turning back to the salad bowl. "Pull him away from the chickens and drag him into the house, Crystal. I want an explanation from him."

"Okay, Mum," I murmured.

I watched Cole pecking at seeds for a few seconds more. Then I made my way out of the kitchen door and crossed the yard to the chicken area.

"Cole?" I called softly. I stepped over the wire fence. *"Cluuuck cluuuck* Cole?"

I really did plan to bring him into the house to Mum.

I really did plan to drag him away from there.

But those seeds looked so delicious!

I bumped some chickens out of the way. Then I dropped down on my knees, lowered my head—and started pecking away.

The next day in school, I don't think I heard a word anyone said. I couldn't stop thinking about the barbecue.

Of course, all of our guests thought what Cole and I did was some kind of a joke. They didn't *get* the joke. But they knew it had to be a joke.

Mum and Dad were really angry. They needed

us to help out. But we were too busy pecking seeds with the chickens.

Later, Mum was really upset when Cole and I refused to eat any of her barbecued chicken. "It was always your favourite!" she cried.

Not any more, I thought sadly.

The idea of eating a chicken made my insides feel as if they were turning inside out!

The next morning, I needed Cole's help in pulling all the feathers from my neck and shoulders. Some big white feathers had poked out of my back, and I couldn't reach them.

It took us each twenty minutes to pluck out all the feathers that had grown during the night. We hid them in my sweater drawer. We didn't want Mum or Dad to see them before we had a chance to explain.

The school day went so slowly. My neck and back kept itching. I prayed that feathers wouldn't grow while I was in school.

And I prayed that none of my teachers would call on me in class. I was clucking more and more. It was becoming a real struggle to talk.

My team had a basketball game in the gym after school against a girls' team from the next county. I had looked forward to it all week. But now I just wanted to hurry home before any kids saw me clucking or pecking seeds from the playground.

I dropped my books in my locker. And I was

sneaking to the front door of the school—when Coach Clay turned the corner. "Crystal, I was *looking* for you!" she cried.

"*Cluck?*" I replied.

"Hilary has a bad cold. I'm going to let you start at forward today," she told me.

"*Cluck—*" I started.

But she didn't give me a chance to reply. She placed her hands on my shoulders, turned me around and marched me to the locker room. "I know you're going to be great," she said. "Go and get changed."

"*Cluck*," I told her. Normally, I'd be really excited! I was going to be the starting forward. This is what I had dreamed about all year!

As I changed into my uniform, the other girls all came over to slap me high fives and wish me good luck.

Maybe I can do it, I told myself. Maybe I will play really well. Maybe I *can* show them just how good a player I am.

But as soon as the game started, I knew I was in trouble.

Big trouble.

Our team won the opening jump. I turned and began running to the other team's basket.

I leaned forward as I ran. My head bobbed up and down.

Up and down. Up and down.

Low clucks escaped my throat.

I tried to straighten up. But I couldn't.

Our centre took a shot. Missed. We all started to run back to the other basket.

"Nooooo," I moaned.

To my horror, I realized that I couldn't run without bobbing my head.

I glanced to the sideline—and saw Coach Clay staring at me. "Crystal—what are you *doing*?" she called.

I heard some kids laughing at me.

"Crystal—stop messing around," Gina, the other forward, scolded me.

The action moved to our opponents' basket, and I ran down court. My head bobbed up and down. I realized I was running stiff-legged. My knees no longer bent!

The ball came sailing towards me.

I couldn't catch it. My hands were tucked under my armpits. My elbows were poked out like wings.

I let out a loud cluck as the ball bounced off my shoulder.

My head bobbed up and down.

My teammates were yelling angrily at me. On the sideline, I saw Coach Clay shaking her head. Girls on the other team were laughing.

Down the court. I tried to pry my hands from my armpits as I ran. My head bobbed. My lips clicked.

I glanced down—and stopped.

No!

My legs.

White feathers were sprouting up and down my legs.

And everyone could see them.

I heard a whistle blow. The referee called time out.

My teammates ran towards our bench. I took of in the other direction. I ran out of the gym and out of the school.

I wanted to run and run and never stop.

I hid in my room during dinner. I was so depressed—and frightened. I wanted to tell

Mum and Dad everything. But what if they didn't believe me? What if they thought it was all a joke?

After dinner, Mum and Dad had to go to school for a Parents Association meeting. Cole and I waited until we heard the car pull away. Then we waddled downstairs to the living room.

We were down on our knees, pecking crumbs in the rug.

My body was covered with white and brown feathers. It would take hours to pull them all off.

"I—*cluuuuck*—I'm so scared," Cole stammered.

"Me, too," I confessed. I pecked at a big ball of fluff.

"Crystal, what are we going to do?" Cole asked softly.

I started to say, "I don't know."

But I suddenly knew exactly what we had to do.

We crept out into a cool, windy night. The swirling wind ruffled my feathers. Up above, a pale half-moon kept sliding behind wispy clouds.

Cole and I walked along the street that led to town. We tried to hurry. But our legs felt stiff, and our knees were hard to bend.

Car headlights swept over the street towards us. We slipped behind a low hedge and hid, clucking softly. We didn't want anyone to see us like this. And we didn't want anyone to ask us where we were going.

We passed through town, making our way along the backs of shops. Trees hissed and shook as the wind picked up. The air grew heavy and moist. I felt a few raindrops on my forehead.

A sweet aroma made me take a deep breath. It came from the bakery. I realized that Mrs Wagner must be baking doughnuts for tomorrow morning.

A sad cry escaped my beak. Would I ever be

able to taste a doughnut again? Or would I spend the rest of my life pecking my food off the ground?

Cole and I turned on to the dirt path that led to Vanessa's old farmhouse. The night grew darker—and colder—as soon as we moved away from town.

Our shoes plodded heavily over the hard dirt path. A few minutes later, I could see the black outline of Vanessa's house against the grey sky.

"What are we *cluuuck* going to say to her?" Cole demanded softly.

I brushed a raindrop off my eyebrow. My hand felt rough and scratchy, my fingers hard as bone.

"I'm going to *bluuuck* tell her how sorry we are," I replied. "I'm going to tell her we didn't mean to knock over her groceries. That it was all a big accident. And we're sorry we didn't stay and help her pick them up. *Cluuuuck*."

We stepped up to Vanessa's wooden fence. The gate had been left open. It banged in the wind.

I raised my eyes to the house. It hung over the tall grass like a low, dark creature. No lights on anywhere.

Had she already gone to sleep?

"I—I don't *bluuuck* think she's home," Cole whispered.

"Of course she's home," I replied sharply.

No answer.

The gate banged behind us. Startled, Cole and I both jumped.

I took a deep breath and pounded my scraggly fist on the door again.

We waited, staring straight ahead. Listening to the harsh whisper of the trees, and to the banging gate.

Silence in the house.

I uttered a sigh of disappointment and turned to my brother. "You were right. Vanessa isn't home."

We backed away from the house. Clouds floated away from the moon. The front window glinted with silvery moonlight.

"Let's peek inside," I urged.

We made our way to the window. Standing on tiptoes, we peered into the living room.

In the silvery light, I stared at the dark shapes of furniture. Old-fashioned, high-back chairs. A long couch covered with pillows. Bookshelves from floor to ceiling.

Everything was very old-looking. But I didn't see anything strange or frightening.

Then a stack of books caught my eye. They were piled on a small, square table beside the couch. The books were big and thick. And even in the pale light, I could see that their covers were old and cracked.

Squinting into the room, I spotted two more of them, lying open on the low coffee table in front of the couch.

"Cole—" I whispered, my heart starting to pound. "See those old books? Do you think they are books about magic?"

"Huh?" He pressed his face against the glass. "What do you mean?"

"You know. *Bluuuck.* Books about magic spells. Sorcery books. They look like they could be old spell books—don't they?"

He nodded. "Yeah. Maybe."

I plucked a white feather from under his chin.

"Owww!" he yelped. "Why'd you do that?"

I shrugged. "Sorry. It was bothering me." I turned my face back to the window and stared at the old books.

"Let's go," Cole urged, tugging my arm. "She isn't here."

"But those books are here," I replied, tugging myself free. "And if they *are* spell books, maybe we could find the right book. You know. *Blu-uuuck*. With the right spell. And we could change *ourselves* back to normal!"

Cole rolled his eyes. He clicked his beak. "Yeah. Sure. Then maybe I'll flap my arms and lay an egg!"

"Don't be sarcastic," I scolded him. "It may be a bad idea. But at least it's an idea."

I pulled him to the front door. I turned the knob—and pushed.

The heavy door creaked open.

"*Bluuuuck*. Let's just take a quick peek at those books," I told my brother, stepping into the cool darkness of the house. "What have we got to lose?"

I pulled Cole into the front hall. The house smelled of coffee and peppery spices. Sort of a sweet-sharp aroma.

I led the way into the living room. Silvery light flooded in through the front window.

The floorboards groaned beneath my shoes. I stopped beside the couch and stared at the pile of old books.

I reached out for the book on top of the stack—when a furious shriek made me stop.

"Ohhh!" I pulled my hand back.

"Vanessa—!" Cole cried.

My breath caught in my chest. My heart skipped a beat.

I spun around—and saw Vanessa's cat leap on to the high back of an old armchair.

The cat's eyes flashed, golden in the pale light. It bared its teeth again in another angry hiss.

"I—I thought it was Vanessa," Cole murmured in a choked voice. "That cat *cluuuuck* doesn't want us here."

"Well, we're not staying long," I told the cat. I motioned for Cole to come over to the couch. "Help me check out these books. If we find the right one . . ."

As Cole passed by the chair, the cat swiped its claws at him.

"Hey—!" Cole ducked away from it.

"Cats don't like chickens," I whispered.

I picked up one of the open books on the coffee table. I raised it close to my face and tried to read the title in the dim light.

The print was smudged. The heavy cover was cracked with age and covered in a layer of dust. "I can't read it," I told Cole.

I saw him move to the wall. "I'll turn on a light," he suggested.

The cat hissed again.

"No—don't!" I called. "No light. If Vanessa comes back, we don't want her to see us."

I rubbed my finger over the title. And tried to focus on it.

"Hey—I don't believe it!" I cried happily.

"What is it, Crystal?" Cole called. "Did you find—"

Before I could answer, the ceiling light flashed on.

"Ohhh!" I cried out when I saw Vanessa standing by the wall.

I stumbled back.

The book dropped from my hand. It thudded heavily on the floor at my feet.

"Vanessa, I—"

I swallowed hard.

And realized I was staring at a painting. A huge oil portrait of Vanessa, hanging on the wall.

"Oh, wow!" I cried. "That painting—it's almost life-sized. I thought—"

I turned to Cole. He stood by the light switch, staring at the big portrait.

"Did *you* click on the light?" I demanded.

"Yes," he replied. "Sorry. I didn't mean to *bluuuck bluuuck* scare you. I thought it would help you read the book title."

The book title!

"Cole—I think I've found the right book!" I cried. "The very first book I picked up."

I bent down and excitedly lifted the old book from the floor.

Yes!

"Cole—look!" I exclaimed, holding up the front cover. "It's called *Chicken Chicken Chicken*. This has to be it! If I can find the spell that Vanessa used inside this book—"

"Then maybe we can reverse it!" Cole cried.

A loud *bang* from the front made us both jump. The black cat screeched and jumped off the chair back. It scurried silently from the room.

"Was that the gate—or was it Vanessa?" I cried.

Cole clicked off the light. We listened, frozen in place. I gripped the old book closely to my chest.

Silence now. Then another bang. Just the gate blowing in the wind.

"Let's get out of here," I whispered, raising my eyes to the front door.

"*Bluuuuck*," Cole replied. He turned and began walking stiff-legged to the door. Even in the dim light, I could see that a thick tuft of feathers had grown on the back of his neck.

Vanessa's cat stood on the hallway floor, arching its back as if ready to attack. We edged past it carefully.

"Nice kitty. Nice kitty," I murmured.

Its angry expression didn't change.

I pushed open the door. The gusting wind caught it and nearly blew it out of my hand.

Cole and I stepped outside. I tugged the door shut.

I carried the heavy book against my chest as we made our way home. We leaned into the wind. My hair fluttered up behind me like a pennant.

Goshen Falls stood in darkness. All of the shops close early. The only bright lights were at the self-service petrol station on the first corner.

Cole and I half-walked, half-trotted down the centre of the street. I couldn't wait to get home and find the spell that Vanessa had used on us.

Finally, our house rose into view. The driveway was still empty. Mum and Dad hadn't returned yet from their meeting at school.

Good! I thought. Maybe I can find the spell and change Cole and me back to normal before they get home.

I led the way up the stairs to my room, still clutching the book to my chest. Cole closed the door behind us.

I dropped on to the edge of my bed and spread the big book on my lap. Cole stood beside me, clucking softly. Staring down at me as I rapidly flipped through the old pages, squinting hard at the tiny type.

"Well?" Cole demanded impatiently. "Is it in there? Is the spell in there?"

I didn't reply. I turned the pages furiously, my eyes running down each column. Faster.

Faster. I turned page after page, my heart pounding.

"Well?" my brother demanded. "Well?"

I slammed the book shut in disgust.

"Noooooo!" I wailed. I tossed the book on to the bed.

"Cole," I cried, shaking my head sadly, "we've made a horrible mistake."

Cole uttered a squawk of horror. The white and brown feathers on the back of his neck stood up on end.

"Crystal—what's wrong?" he choked out.

"It's the wrong book!" I cried, jumping up from the bed. I left a pile of feathers where I'd been sitting. "It's a *cookbook*! It's a whole book of chicken recipes!"

"Yuck!" Cole cried.

The idea sent a wave of nausea up from my stomach. My arms suddenly itched. I gazed down and saw white feathers curling up from the skin.

"We have to go back there," I told my brother. My beak clicked loudly. It stretched out in front of my chin now. My teeth were sinking into my gums, about to disappear completely. I really had to struggle to form words.

Cole swallowed hard. "Go back?"

"Before it's too late," I whispered. "Before

we're completely chicken—not human at all."

He gulped and didn't reply.

I hoisted up the book and started waddling to the bedroom door. I stopped in shock when I glimpsed my reflection in the dresser mirror.

My eyes! My head!

My eyes had changed into small, round circles. And the shape of my head was changing, too. Growing narrow. My eyes were far apart now, moving to the sides of my head.

"No! Oh, noooooo!" I opened my beak in a mournful wail.

"Come on—let's hurry!" Cole urged. He grabbed my hand. Feathers brushed feathers. The backs of our hands had sprouted a thick layer of short, white feathers.

"Yes. Hurry!" I repeated, bobbing my head up and down.

We made our way down the stairs and out the door. Back out into the dark, wind-swirled night.

I had a strong urge to bend down and peck some gravel from the driveway. But I fought it off and trotted to the street.

We had to hurry back there. Back to Vanessa's house.

Would we make it in time?

The trip was normally a ten-minute walk. But it took Cole and me much longer. Partly because our chicken legs were so stiff. And partly because it's a lot harder to see where you're going when your eyes are on different sides of your head!

The gusting winds softened a little as we finally reached Vanessa's farmhouse. Pale moonlight cast shadows over the broken shingled roof.

The windows were still dark. We leaned on the fence, catching our breath and studying the house. No sign that she had returned home.

Clutching the heavy recipe book to my chest, I pushed past the gate and led the way to the front door. Once again, it opened easily. Cole and I stepped inside, inhaling the strange, spicy fragrance of the house.

"*Cluuuuck*, Vanessa?" I called. "Hello? Anyone home?"

A pair of yellow eyes glared at us from the banister. The black cat let out a yawn. Not at all surprised to see us back. And from the way it stared at us, not at all pleased to have its home invaded once again.

"She isn't here," Cole whispered. "Let's *bluuuck bluuuck* hurry."

I dropped the recipe book on the coffee table and turned to the stack of books beside the couch. As I turned, a bowl on the coffee table caught my attention.

Sunflower seeds!

I couldn't resist. I poked my head into the bowl and began sucking the tasty seeds into my beak.

"Crystal—what are you *doing*?" Cole cried in a hoarse whisper. "Get away from there!"

He grabbed a book from the stack and began frantically pawing through it. I pecked up a few more seeds. Then I grabbed a book, too.

Cole let out a triumphant squawk. "These books—they're all magic books!" he declared.

"You're *bluuuck* right," I agreed. "Hundreds and hundreds of magic spells."

Cole flipped rapidly through the pages of his book. His eyes were practically spinning! "How will we ever find the right one?" he demanded.

"I think I just found it," I told him.

I carried the book to the window and held it up to the moonlight to see it better.

Yes!

"What does it say?" Cole asked excitedly. He dropped his book and came bobbing across the room to me.

"It's a whole *cluuuck* page of chicken spells," I replied, holding the book up to the window. "This one is called 'Human into Chicken'. That sounds right—doesn't it?"

"No. Find 'Chicken into Human'!" Cole exclaimed.

My eyes swept over the pages. "No such

thing," I told him. "We'll just have to reverse the 'Human into Chicken' spell."

"Well, go ahead!" he cried, his feathery head bobbing up and down excitedly. "Reverse it! Do it! What do we have to do?"

I saw that he was so excited, he couldn't stand still. He tucked his hands under his armpits, stuck out his elbows to form wings—and began clucking round and round in a circle.

"Cole—*bluuuck bluuck bluuuck*!" I scolded.

He ignored me and kept clucking away. Flapping his arms and making a small circle over the floor.

I turned back to the book and carefully read the spell. It didn't look too hard. It didn't call for any special ingredients. It was just a bunch of words that had to be said rapidly. And the spell caster had to cluck a lot and do a simple dance.

Then, according to the book, you point at the poor victims and whisper, "Chicken chicken!"

Just as Vanessa had done to us.

"It looks pretty easy," I told Cole. "Stop dancing around, and I'll *bluuuck* try it."

He stopped his frantic flapping and circling. He turned to me. "Don't forget to *cluuuck bluuck*," he called.

I knew what he meant. He was reminding me to do the spell *backwards*.

Hmm . . . I glanced over the spell. That wasn't

going to be so easy. But I had no choice. I had to try it.

Balancing the heavy, old book in one hand, I pointed to Cole, then to myself, with my free hand. "Chicken chicken," I whispered.

Okay. That was the very end of the spell.

I lowered my eyes to the bottom of the page. And I started to read the words, going up: "Cluck cluck chick. Chick cluck cluck chick."

The spell instructed me to take three steps forward and two to the right. So I took two steps to the left, then three steps back.

I moved my scrawny chicken finger over the words, being careful to read them in reverse order:

"Chick cluck chick cluck. Cluck cluck chick."

Then, following the instructions backwards, I took two giant steps, then three steps to the right. I flapped my arms and clucked four times.

Then I read the *first* words of the spell at the top of the page: "Cluck cluck chick cluck. Cluck chick cluck."

That was it.

That was the whole spell. I had done it completely backwards.

Would it work? Would reversing Vanessa's spell turn Cole and me back to normal?

Would it do anything at all?

Yes.

Suddenly, I began to feel strange. My arms

and legs began to itch like crazy. The feathers up and down my arms shot straight out.

The book fell from my hand and thudded loudly to the floor.

Egg-shaped spots sparkled in front of my eyes.

When the spots faded, the room turned purple and started to tilt.

"Hey—something is happening!" Cole cried in a tiny voice. He sounded far, far away.

Yes, something is happening, I agreed, grabbing the window ledge to keep from falling.

Something is happening.

But what?

I felt so dizzy. The room rocked and swayed.

The floor suddenly appeared so far away. I blinked. Once. Twice.

The floor still seemed a mile below.

"*Cluck cluck*, Cole—?" I turned to my brother. Then I let out a shrill squawk of horror.

Now I knew why the floor seemed so far down. Cole and I had GROWN!

We weren't chickens any more. We were BIIIIIG chickens!

"I—I'm as big as a *horse*!" I cried.

I gazed up. The ceiling was only an centimetre or two above my head.

Cole uttered a startled moan. His whole body trembled. Enormous feathers shook free and fell to the floor. He flapped his arms, and more feathers tumbled off him.

I saw Vanessa's black cat back into the hall-way. Its yellow eyes were wide with fear. It arched its back and raised its tail and hissed at us furiously.

I took a step towards Cole. My big, feathery body bobbed in front of me. "I—I must have *bluuuuuck* done something wrong!" I told my brother.

Cole hopped up and down, bobbing his head. He clicked his beak, but no sound came out. Finally, he choked out, "Crystal—try again."

Yes. He was right. I had to try to reverse the spell again.

Maybe I couldn't turn us back into humans. But I might be able to shrink us back to our normal size.

I bent over to find the book on the floor. It was hard to find. I was so tall, the book looked about the size of a CD case!

It wasn't easy to pick it up, either. It kept sliding out from my scraggly chicken fingers.

It seemed like *hours* before I managed to find the spell again. Then I raised the little book up close to my right eye and began to perform the spell backwards once again.

Please, please, I prayed. *Let me get it right this time. Please, let Vanessa's spell reverse itself.*

I finished up with the final: "Cluck cluck chick cluck. Cluck chick cluck."

Would it work?

I heard Cole let out a choked cluck from across the room.

Once again, I began to feel weird. The egg-shaped spots sparkled in front of my eyes, blinding me with their brightness.

I shut my eyes.

I could feel the room tilting and swaying.

I tried to grab hold of something. But my hands grasped only air.

"Ooooh!" I let out a low moan as I felt myself start to fall. Yes. I was falling . . . falling . . .

When I opened my eyes, I didn't know where I was. The room had disappeared. I was surrounded by darkness. Surrounded by . . .

Whoa!

I gazed up at the book. The book of spells—it rested beside me on the floor. But it had grown! The book was taller than me!

"Cheep cheep!" I cried.

"Cheep cheep cheep," I heard Cole's tiny reply.

I spun around to find him. "Cheep?"

"Cheep cheep!"

He was a little yellow chick! I swallowed hard. I knew what that meant. That meant that I was *also* a tiny yellow chick!

I had reversed the spell—too much!

I struggled to speak—but I could only make a tiny *cheep cheep* sound. My tiny feet clicked on the wooden floor.

"Cheep cheep?" Cole asked. The poor little guy sounded so frightened.

My tiny heart was pounding in my feathery yellow chest. I suddenly felt so angry. Why was this happening to us? Why did Vanessa think she had a right to do this to us?

I pecked my little beak furiously against the floor. I had no other way of letting out my anger.

But I didn't have much time to be angry.

A dark blur of motion made me raise my eyes.

I saw the giant shadow. No! It was Vanessa's cat. The cat perched on the desk next to an old-fashioned-looking typewriter.

Its tail smacked the typewriter as the cat dropped to the floor.

It crossed the room quickly, silently—and rose up over me, its eyes glowing with excitement.

It pulled back its lips, revealing its enormous teeth.

"Cheep cheep!" I squeaked. I froze in fear.

The cat pounced.

I felt its front paws wrap around my tiny, soft body.

Then the paws began to squeeze.

I tried to kick. I tried to thrash my arms. Tried to wriggle free.

But I was helpless against the giant cat.

Its big paws squeezed me until I could barely breathe.

Then it grabbed my head in its paws.

And lifted me—up. Up.

The cat dangled me in the air for a few seconds.

I wanted to scream.

I wanted to break free.

But I was helpless. Too weak and tiny to do anything.

The cat's eyes flashed as it dangled me in front of its face. Then it opened its mouth wide—and stuffed me inside.

Ohhhh. The cat's hot breath roared over me. The inside of its mouth felt so hot, so disgustingly sticky and wet.

"Cheep cheep cheeeep!" I squealed.

The cat bounced me around on its tongue.

And then—to my surprise—spat me out.

I fell hard on to my side on the floor. Behind me, I could hear Cole cheeping weakly.

I scrambled to my feet. I wanted to run.

But the cat grabbed me again. Lifted me high off the floor in its rough paws.

I saw the cat's head, tilted at an angle. I saw a gleam of silvery drool on its fangs. Felt its hot, sour breath roll over me once again.

The cat raised me high. Higher.

Is it going to swallow me this time? I wondered.

Is it going to shove me into its mouth and swallow me?

No. The purring creature let me drop back to the floor.

I landed on my back. My tiny feet clawed the air.

Before I could scramble to my feet, the cat picked me up again—this time by the foot. It swung me from side to side in front of its open mouth.

It's *playing* with me, I realized.

The cat is playing with its food!

And when it's finished playing . . . *then* it will eat me!

I could hear Cole cheeping down on the floor. The cat held me in one paw, dangling me in front of its face. Then it began batting me with its other paw, making me spin.

The spinning made me dizzy. I shut my eyes as the cat dropped me once again to the floor.

I landed on my side and lay there. I felt so weak, so frightened, I didn't even try to move.

Panting hard, I waited for the cat to pounce again. Waited to feel its claws wrap around me. Waited to be lifted into the air again.

Waited . . .

When it didn't pounce, I lifted my head. I struggled to focus.

Where was it?

I could hear my brother cheeping in terror somewhere across the floor.

I climbed slowly to my feet. I ruffled my feathers, which were wet and sticky from being inside the cat's mouth.

Where was the cat? Why did it stop torturing me?

The lights flashed on.

"Eeeeep!" I uttered a shrill shriek as a big face lowered itself towards me.

Vanessa!

"Well, well!" her voice boomed in my tiny ears. "What have we here?"

Her hand swooped down and grabbed me off the floor.

She scooped me up, then picked up Cole, too. She perched us in the palm of her hand and held us close to her pale face. A pleased smile spread across her black-lipsticked lips.

"I see you found my spell book, little chickies," she teased. "Let me guess. You must be Crystal and Cole."

Cole and I cheeped loudly and hopped up and down in protest. Vanessa laughed. "You're both so cute!" she exclaimed. "What a shame I had to teach you a lesson." She tsk-tsked.

"Cheep cheep!" I squeaked.

I wanted to ask why she had done this to Cole and me. I wanted to promise her that no matter what it was we had done—we'd never do it again. I wanted to demand that she change us back—now.

But all I could do was *cheep*!

"What should I do with you two?" Vanessa asked, her dark eyes flashing. "Should I send you back out? It's a long way to your house from here. You'd probably be *eaten* before you got there."

"Cheeeeep!" Cole and I pleaded.

How could we communicate with her? How could we talk to her? How?

I suddenly had an idea.

The old typewriter on the desk. Vanessa was holding Cole and me right above it.

I glanced down. A sheet of white paper lay curled in the typewriter. Yes! I thought. Yes! Our only chance.

I didn't take another second to think about it.

I leaped from Vanessa's palm. And landed with a hard *plop* on the desktop.

"Hey, chickie—!" I heard Vanessa's startled cry. She lowered her hand to pick me up again.

But I jumped on to the typewriter keys. Lowered my head. And began pecking away with my hard little beak.

I pecked a V. Then I hopped up to the left and pecked an A. As Vanessa's hand swooped to grab me, I slid back down to the bottom row and pecked an N.

Vanessa's hand stopped centimetres above me. Could she see what I was doing? Did she figure out that I was typing her a message?

The E was nearly at the top of the keyboard. I stumbled on the keys and nearly typed the wrong letter. But I hit the E, then backed up a step and pecked two S's.

I glanced up. Yes! She was watching. She had Cole resting in her palm. She leaned over the desk, and her dark eyes stared down at the sheet of paper.

I was gasping for breath by the time I finished. My little heart was pounding. It was such hard work! But I typed the whole message:

VANESSA, WE'RE REALLY SORRY. WE DIDN'T MEAN TO SPILL YOUR GROCERIES. WE CAME TO APOLOGIZE.

I dropped weakly on to the desktop. So exhausted, I could barely move.

I turned and raised my eyes to Vanessa.

Would she help us? Would she accept our apology? Would she change us back to normal?

Vanessa brought her face down close to me. "Your apology is a little too late," she said coldly. "There's nothing I can do."

Cole uttered a pitiful "Cheep".

I raised myself up with a sigh. Then I stumbled back wearily on to the typewriter keys.

PLEAS, I pecked out.

I was so tired, I didn't have the strength to push down the E at the end.

I gazed up hopefully at Vanessa. She stared down at the word I had typed. She tapped her chin with her black fingernails.

"Well . . ." she said finally. "I like the way you say *'please'*." She lifted me up gently and set me down in her palm beside Cole.

"Politeness is so important," Vanessa said, holding us up to her face. "Especially for young people. That's what I care about more than anything else in the world. Good manners."

Her dark eyes narrowed at us. "That day in front of the grocery," she scolded, "you didn't apologize for crashing into me. So I had no

109

choice. I had to punish you." She studied us, tsk-tsking.

So *that's* why Anthony wasn't turned into a chicken, too! I realized. Before he ran away, Anthony had called out to Vanessa that he was sorry.

If only Cole and I had apologized then! We wouldn't be peeping little chicks today.

But how were we to know that Vanessa was such a manners freak?

She carried us over to a tall bookshelf and held us close to the books. "Do you see my collection?" she asked. "All etiquette books. Dozens and dozens of manners books. I have dedicated my life to manners."

She gazed at us sternly. "If only kids today weren't so rude. I wish I could help you two. I really do. But your apology came too late. Far too late."

She set us both down on the desk. I guess her hand was getting tired. She rubbed it tenderly with her other hand.

Now what? I wondered.

Was she going to send us home like this? Vanessa was right. Cole and I would never make it. Some dog or cat or raccoon would turn us into dinner before we went a block or two.

I cheeped in panic. My tiny feathers stood straight up. What could we do?

I had one last, desperate idea.

One more time, I climbed on to the typewriter keyboard. And I began to type . . .

THANK YOU FOR EXPLAINING TO US. AND THANK YOU FOR TRYING TO TEACH US TO BE POLITE. YOURS TRULY, COLE AND CRYSTAL

I *said* it was a desperate idea. About as desperate as a chicken can get. But I stared up at Vanessa, watching her read it. Hoping . . . hoping . . .

"I don't *believe* it!" Vanessa exclaimed. She tore the sheet of paper from the typewriter and read it again. "A thank-you note!" she cried. "You wrote me a thank-you note!"

She gazed down at Cole and me with a broad smile. "No kids today *ever* write thank-you notes!" she cried. "This is the politest thing I've ever seen!"

She danced around with it. "A thank-you note! An actual thank-you note!"

And then she turned. Pointed a finger at Cole, then at me. Mumbled some words. And pointed again.

"Whooooa!" I cried, feeling my body grow. I felt like a balloon inflating. The little yellow feathers fell away. My hair grew back. My arms . . . my hands!

"YAAAAAY!" I cried. Cole joined my happy cheer.

We were back! Vanessa had changed us back—to *us*!

We pinched each other, just to make sure. Then we tossed back our heads and laughed. We were so happy!

Vanessa laughed, too. We all laughed gleefully together.

Then Vanessa turned and started towards the kitchen. "Let me get you both a drink," she offered. "I know how thirsty these spells can make a person."

"Thank you!" I cried, remembering how important politeness was to Vanessa.

"Yes—thank you!" Cole added loudly.

We grinned at each other. We pinched each other again. Skin! Real skin—with no feathers!

I moved my lips. I licked them with my tongue. Soft, human lips that didn't click.

Vanessa returned with two glasses of cola. "I know kids like cola," she said. She handed a glass to me and a glass to Cole. "Drink up," she urged. "You've been through a lot."

I *did* feel terribly thirsty. I took a few long sips of the cola. It felt cold and tingly on my tongue. Wonderful! Better than seeds off the carpet.

Wow. I was so happy to be me again.

I raised my eyes and saw Cole tilt his glass to his mouth and drink the cola down. He was really thirsty!

When he finished, he lowered his glass—and let out the loudest burp I'd ever heard!

Cole burst out laughing.

I couldn't help myself.

It was such a funny burp, I started laughing, too.

I was still laughing when Vanessa stepped in front of me.

What is her problem? I wondered.

Then she pointed her finger, first at Cole, then at me. And whispered, "Pig pig."

Goosebumps

Don't Go To Sleep!

Klonk! "Ow! The Klingon got me!"

I rubbed my head and kicked my life-sized photo of a Klingon—one of those warlike aliens on *Star Trek*—out of the way. I'd been reaching for one of my favourite books, *Ant Attack on Pluto*, when the big hunk of cardboard fell off the top shelf and klonked me on the head.

I kicked the Klingon again. "Take that, you evil piece of cardboard!"

I was fed up. My stuff kept attacking me.

My room was packed with junk. Things were always leaping off the walls and whacking me on the head. This wasn't the first time.

"Uhn!" I gave the Klingon another kick for good measure.

"Matthew Amsterdam, twelve-year-old geek." My older brother, Greg, stood in my bedroom doorway, murmuring into a tape recorder.

"Get out of my room!" I grumbled.

Greg totally ignored me. He always does.

"Matt is skinny, small for his age, with a

round, pig-like baby face," he said. He was still talking into the tape recorder.

"Matt's hair is so blond that, from a distance, he almost looks bald." Greg spoke in a deep, fake voice. He was trying to sound like the guy who describes animals on those nature shows.

"At least I don't have a Brillo pad sitting on my head," I cracked.

Greg and my sister, Pam, both have wiry brown hair. Mine is white-blond and really thin. Mum says my dad had the same hair as me. But I don't remember him. He died when I was a baby.

Greg smirked at me and went on in that *Wild Kingdom* voice. "Matt's natural habitat is a small bedroom filled with science fiction books, models of alien spacecraft, comic books, dirty socks, rotten pizza crusts, and other geekazoid stuff. How can Matt can stand it? Scientists are puzzled by this. Remember, geeks have always been a mystery to normal humans."

"I'd rather be a geek than a nerd like you," I said.

"You're not smart enough to be a nerd," he shot back in his regular voice.

My sister, Pam, appeared beside him in the doorway. "What's happening here in Geek World?" she asked. "Did the mother ship finally come for you, Matt?"

I threw *Ant Attack on Pluto* at her.

Pam is in tenth grade. Greg is in eleventh. They gang up on me all the time.

Greg spoke into his tape recorder again. "When threatened, the geek *will* attack. However, he is about as dangerous as a bowl of mashed potatoes."

"Get out!" I yelled. I tried to close the door, but they blocked it.

"I can't leave," Greg protested. "I have a school project. I have to watch everybody in the family and write a paper about how they act. It's for social studies."

"Go and watch Pam pick her nose," I snapped.

Pam knocked Greg aside and pushed her way into the room. She grabbed me by the neck of my *Star Trek* T-shirt.

"Take that back!" she ordered.

"Let go!" I cried. "You're stretching out my shirt!"

"Matthew is very touchy about his geek clothes," Greg mumbled into the recorder.

"I said take that back!" Pam shook me. "Or I'll set Biggie on you!"

Biggie is our dog. He's not big—he's a dachshund. But he hates me for some reason.

With everybody else—even total strangers— he wags his tail, licks their hands, the whole bit. With me, he growls and snaps.

Once Biggie sneaked into my room and bit me in my sleep. I'm a heavy sleeper—it takes a lot to wake me up. But believe me, when a dog bites you, you wake up.

"Here, Biggie!" Pam called.

"Okay!" I cried. "I take it back."

"Good answer," Pam said. "You win the noogie prize!" She started knocking me on the head.

"Ow! Ow!" I gasped.

"The geek's sister gives him noogies to the head," Greg commented. "Geek says, 'Ow!'"

Finally Pam let me go. I stumbled and collapsed on my bed. The bed knocked against the wall. A pile of books rained down on me from the shelf over my head.

"Give me that tape recorder for a second," Pam said to Greg. She snatched it from him and yelled into the microphone. "The geek is down! Thanks to me, Pamela Amsterdam, the world is safe for cool people again! Woo! Woo! Woo!"

I hate my life.

Pam and Greg use me as their human punch bag. Maybe if Mum were around more, she'd be able to stop them.

But she is hardly ever around. She has two jobs. Her day job is teaching people how to use computers. And her night job is typing at a law firm.

Pam and Greg are supposed to be taking care of me. They take care of me, all right.

They make sure I'm miserable twenty-four hours a day.

"This room stinks," Pam groaned. "Let's get out of here, Greg."

They slammed the door behind them. My model space shuttle fell off the dresser and crashed to the floor.

At least they left me alone. I didn't care what mean things they said, as long as they went away.

I settled on my bed to read *Ant Attack on Pluto*. I'd much rather be on the planet Pluto than in my own house—even with giant ants shooting spit rays at me.

My bed felt lumpy. I shoved a bunch of books and clothes to the floor.

I had the smallest bedroom in the house—of course. I always got the worst of everything. Even the guest room was bigger than my room.

I didn't understand it. I needed a big room more than anybody! I had so many books, posters, models and other junk that there was barely room for me to sleep.

I opened my book and started reading. I came to a really scary part. Justin Case, a human space traveller, was captured by the evil ant emperor. The ant emperor closed in on him, closer, closer . . .

I shut my eyes for a second—just a second— but I guess I fell asleep. Suddenly I felt the ant emperor's hot, stinking breath on my face!

Ugh! It smelled exactly like dog food.

Then I heard growling.

I opened my eyes.

It was worse than I thought. Worse than an ant emperor.

It was Biggie—ready to spring!

"Biggie!" I screamed. "Get off me!"

Snap! He attacked me with his gaping dachshund jaws.

I dodged him—he missed me. I shoved him off the bed.

He snarled at me and tried to jump back up. He was too short. He couldn't reach the bed without taking a running leap.

I stood on the bed. Biggie snapped at my feet. "Help!" I yelled.

That's when I saw Pam and Greg in the doorway, laughing their heads off.

Biggie backed up to take his running jump. "Help me, you guys!" I begged.

"Yeah, right," Pam said. Greg doubled over laughing.

"Come on," I whined. "I can't get down! He'll bite me!"

Greg gasped for breath. "Why do you think we put him on your bed in the first place? Ha-ha-ha-ha!"

"You shouldn't sleep so much, Matt," Greg said. "We thought we had to wake you up."

"Besides, we were bored," Pam added. "We wanted to have some fun."

Biggie galloped across the room and leapt on to the bed. As he jumped up, I jumped down. I scurried across the floor—slipping on comic books as I ran.

Biggie raced after me. I ducked into the hallway and slammed the door just before he got out.

Biggie barked like crazy.

"Let him out, Matt!" Pam scolded me. "How can you be so mean to poor, sweet Biggie?"

"Leave me alone!" I shouted. I ran downstairs to the living room. I plopped myself on the couch and flicked on the TV. I didn't bother to surf— I always watch the same channel. The Sci-Fi channel.

I heard Biggie bounding down the steps. I tensed, waiting for him to attack. But he waddled into the kitchen.

Probably going to eat some disgusting doggie treats, I thought. The fat little monster.

The front door opened. Mum came in, balancing a couple of bags of groceries.

"Hi, Mum!" I cried. I was glad she was home. Pam and Greg cooled it a little when she was around.

"Hi, honey." She carried the bags into the

kitchen. "There's my little Biggie!" she cooed. "How's my sweet little pup?"

Everybody loves Biggie except for me.

"Greg!" Mum called. "It's your turn to make dinner tonight!"

"I can't!" Greg yelled from upstairs. "Mum— I've got so much homework to do! I can't get the dinner tonight."

Sure. He was so busy doing his homework, he couldn't stop driving me crazy.

"Make Matt do it," Pam shouted. "He's not doing anything. He's just watching TV."

"I have homework too, you know," I protested.

Greg came down the steps. "Right," he said. "Seventh-grade homework is *so* tough."

"I'll bet you didn't think it was easy when *you* were in seventh grade."

"Boys, please don't fight," Mum said. "I've only got a couple of hours before I have to go back to work. Matt, start dinner. I'm going to go upstairs and lie down for a few minutes."

I stormed into the kitchen. "Mum! It's not my turn!"

"Greg will cook another night," Mum promised.

"What about Pam?"

"Matt—that's enough. You're cooking. That's final." She dragged herself upstairs to her bedroom.

"Rats!" I muttered. I opened a cabinet door

and slammed it shut. "I never get my way around here!"

"What are you making for dinner, Matt?" Greg asked. "Geek burgers?"

"Matthew Amsterdam chews with his mouth open." Greg was talking into his stupid tape recorder again. We were all in the kitchen, eating dinner.

"Tonight the Amsterdams have tuna casserole for dinner," he said. "Matt defrosted it. He left it in the oven too long. The noodles on the bottom are burned."

"Shut up," I muttered.

Nobody said anything for a few minutes. The only sounds were forks clicking against plates and Biggie's toenails on the kitchen floor.

"How was school today, kids?" Mum asked.

"Mrs Amsterdam asks her children about their day," Greg said to the tape recorder.

"Greg, do you have to do that at the dinner table?" Mum sighed.

"Mrs Amsterdam complains about her son Greg's behaviour," Greg murmured.

"Greg!"

"Greg's mother's voice gets louder. Could she be angry?"

"GREG!"

"I have to do it, Mum," Greg insisted in his normal voice. "It's for school!"

"It's getting on my nerves," Mum said.

"Mine too," I chimed in.

"Who asked you, Matt?" Greg snapped.

"So cut it out until after dinner, okay?" Mum asked.

Greg didn't say anything. But he put the tape recorder on the table and started to eat.

Pam said, "Mum, can I put my winter clothes in the wardrobe in the guest room? My wardrobe is packed."

"I'll think about it," Mum said.

"Hey!" I cried. "She has a huge wardrobe! Her wardrobe is almost as big as my whole room!"

"So?" Pam sneered.

"My room is the smallest one in the house!" I protested. "I can hardly walk through it."

"That's because you're a slob," Pam cracked.

"I'm not a slob! I'm neat! But I need a bigger bedroom. Mum, can I move into the guest room?"

Mum shook her head. "No."

"But why not?"

"I want to keep that room nice for guests," Mum explained.

"What guests?" I cried. "We never have any guests!"

"Your grandparents come every Christmas."

"That's once a year. Grandma and Grandpa won't mind sleeping in my little room once a year. The rest of the time they've got a whole house to themselves!"

"Your room is too small to sleep two people," Mum said. "I'm sorry, Matt. You can't have the guest room."

"Mum!"

"What do you care where you sleep, anyway?" Pam said. "You are the best sleeper in the world. You could sleep through a hurricane!"

Greg picked up the tape recorder. "When Matt isn't propped up in front of the TV, he is usually sleeping. He is asleep more than he's awake."

"Mum, Greg talked into the tape recorder again," I tattled.

"I know," Mum said wearily. "Greg, put it down."

"Mum, please let me switch rooms. I need a bigger room! I don't just sleep in my room—I *live* there! I need a place to get away from Pam and Greg. Mum—you don't know what it's like when you're not here! They're so mean to me!"

"Matt, stop it," Mum replied. "You have a wonderful brother and sister, and they take good care of you. You should appreciate them."

"I hate them!"

"Matt! I've had enough of this! Go to your room!"

"There's no room for me in there!" I cried.

"Now!"

As I ran upstairs to my room, I heard Greg

say in his tape recorder voice, "Matt has been punished. His crime? Being a geek."

I slammed the door, stuffed my face in a pillow, and screamed.

I spent the rest of the evening in my room.

"It's not fair!" I muttered to myself. "Pam and Greg get whatever they want—and I get punished!"

Nobody is using the guest room, I thought. I don't care what Mum says. *I'm* sleeping there from now on.

Mum left for her night job. I waited until I heard Pam and Greg turn out the lights and go to their rooms. Then I slipped out of my room and into the guest room.

I was going to sleep in that guest room. And nothing was going to stop me.

I didn't think it was that big a deal. What was the worst thing that could happen? Mum might get mad at me. So what?

I had no idea that when I woke up in the morning, my life would be a complete disaster.

My feet were cold. That was the first thing I noticed when I woke up.

They were sticking out from under the covers. I sat up and tossed the blanket down over them.

Then I pulled the blanket back up. Were those my feet?

They were huge. Not monster huge, but huge for me. Way bigger than they'd been the day before.

Man, I thought. I'd heard about growth spurts. I knew kids grew fast at my age. But this was ridiculous!

I crept out of the guest room. I could hear Mum and Pam and Greg downstairs, eating breakfast.

Oh, no, I thought. I've overslept. I hope no one noticed that I didn't sleep in my room last night.

I went to the bathroom to brush my teeth. Everything felt a little weird.

When I touched the bathroom doorknob, it

seemed to be in the wrong place. As if someone had lowered it during the night. The ceiling felt lower too.

I turned on the light and glanced in the mirror.

Was that me?

I couldn't stop staring at myself. I looked like myself—and I didn't.

My face wasn't so round. I touched my upper lip. It was covered with blond fuzz. And I was about fifteen centimetres taller than I'd been the day before!

I—I was *older*. I looked about sixteen years old!

No, no, I thought. This can't be right. I've got to be imagining this.

I'll just close my eyes for a minute. When I open them, I'll be twelve again.

I squeezed my eyes shut. I counted to ten.

I opened my eyes.

Nothing had changed.

I was a teenager!

My heart began to pound. I'd read that old story about Rip Van Winkle. He goes to sleep for a hundred years. When he wakes up, everything is different.

Had that happened to me? I wondered. Had I just slept for four years straight?

I hurried downstairs to find Mum. She'd tell me what was going on.

I raced downstairs in my pyjamas. I wasn't used to having such big feet. On the third step, I tripped over my left foot.

"Noooo!"

Thud!

I rolled the rest of the way down.

I landed on my face in front of the kitchen. Greg and Pam cracked up—of course.

"Nice one, Matt!" Greg said. "Ten points!"

I dragged myself to my feet. I had no time for Greg's jokes. I had to talk to Mum.

She sat at the kitchen table, eating eggs.

"Mum!" I cried. "Look at me!"

She looked at me. "I see you. You're not dressed yet. You'd better hurry or you'll be late for school."

"But, Mum!" I insisted. "I'm—I'm a teenager!"

"I'm all too well aware of that," Mum said. "Now hurry up. I'm leaving in fifteen minutes."

"Yeah, hurry up, Matt," Pam piped up. "You'll make us late for school."

I turned to snap back at her—but stopped. She and Greg sat at the table, munching cereal.

Nothing weird about that, right?

The only thing was, they looked different too. If I was sixteen, Pam and Greg should have been nineteen and twenty.

But they weren't. They weren't even fifteen and sixteen.

They looked eleven and twelve!

They'd got younger!

"This is impossible!" I screeched.

"This is impossible!" Greg echoed, making fun of me.

Pam started giggling.

"Mum—listen to me!" I cried. "Something weird is going on. Yesterday I was twelve—and today I'm sixteen!"

"*You're* the weirdo!" Greg joked. He and Pam were cracking up. They were just as obnoxious now as they were when they were older.

Mum was only half-listening to me. I shook her arm to get her attention.

"Mum! Pam and Greg are my *older* brother and sister! But now suddenly they're younger! Don't you remember? Greg is the oldest!"

"Matt has gone cuckoo!" Greg cracked. "Cuckoo! Cuckoo!"

Pam fell on the floor laughing.

Mum stood up and set her plate in the sink.

"Matt, I don't have time for this. Go upstairs and get dressed right now."

"But, Mum—"

"Now!"

What could I do? Nobody would listen to me. They all acted as if everything was normal.

I went upstairs and got dressed for school. I couldn't find my old clothes. My drawers were full of clothes I'd never seen before. They all fit my new, bigger body.

Could this be some kind of joke? I wondered as I laced up my size-ten trainers.

Greg must be playing some crazy trick on me.

But how? How could Greg get me to grow—and get himself to shrink?

Even Greg couldn't do that.

Then Biggie trotted in.

"Oh, no," I cried. "Stay away, Biggie. Stay away!"

Biggie didn't listen. He ran right up to me—and licked me on the leg.

He didn't growl. He didn't bite. He wagged his tail.

That's it! I realized. Everything has really gone crazy.

"Matt! We're leaving!" Mum called.

I hurried downstairs and out the front door. Everybody else was already in the car.

Mum drove us to school. She pulled up in front of my school, Madison Middle School. I started to get out of the car.

"Matt!" Mum scolded. "Where are you going? Get back in here!"

"I'm going to school!" I explained. "I thought you wanted me to go to school!"

"Bye, Mum!" Pam chirped. She and Greg kissed Mum goodbye and hopped out of the car.

They ran into the school building.

"Stop fooling around, Matt," Mum said. "I'm going to be late for work."

I got back into the car. Mum drove another couple of miles. She stopped . . . in front of the high school.

"Here you are, Matt," Mum said.

I gulped. High school!

"But I'm not ready for high school!" I protested.

"What is your problem today?" Mum snapped. She reached across the front seat and opened my door. "Get going!"

I had to get out. I had no choice.

"Have a good day!" she called as she pulled away.

One look at that school and I knew—I was *not* going to have a good day.

A bell rang. Big, scary-looking kids poured into the school building.

"Come on, kid. Let's move it." A teacher pushed me towards the door.

My stomach lurched. This was like the first day of school—times ten! Times a zillion!

I wanted to scream: I can't go to high school! I'm only in the seventh grade!

I wandered through the halls with hundreds of other kids. Where do I go? I wondered. I don't even know what class I'm in!

A big guy wearing a football jacket marched up to me and stuck his face in my face.

"Um, hello," I said. Who was this guy?

He didn't move. He didn't say a word. He just stood there, nose to nose with me.

"Um, listen," I began. "I don't know what class to go to. Do you know where they keep the kids who are about—you know—my age?"

The big—very, very big—guy opened his mouth.

"You little creep," he muttered. "I'm going to get you for what you did to me yesterday."

"Me?" My heart fluttered. What was he talking about? "*I* did something to *you*? I don't think so. I didn't do anything to you! I wasn't even here yesterday!"

He laid his huge paws on my shoulders—and squeezed.

"Ow!" I cried.

"Today, after school," he said slowly. "You're going to get it."

He let me go and walked slowly down the hall as if he owned the place.

I was so scared, I dived into the first classroom I came to.

I sat at the back. A tall woman with dark, curly hair stepped in front of the blackboard.

"All right, people!" she yelled. Everybody quietened down. "Open your books to page one hundred and fifty-seven."

What class is this? I wondered. I watched as the girl next to me pulled a textbook out of her bag. I looked at the cover.

No. Oh, no.

It couldn't be.

The title of the book was *Advanced Maths*: *Calculus*.

Calculus! I'd never even heard of that!

I was bad at maths—even seventh-grade maths. How could I do calculus?

The teacher spotted me and narrowed her eyes.

"Matt? Are you supposed to be in this class?"

"No!" I cried, jumping up from my seat. "I'm not supposed to be in this class, that's for sure!"

The teacher added, "You're in my two-thirty class, Matt. Unless you need to switch?"

"No, no! That's okay." I started backing out of the room. "I got mixed up, that's all!"

I hurried out of there as fast as I could. Close one, I thought. I won't be back at two-thirty, either.

I think I'll cut maths class today.

Now what do I do? I wondered. I wandered down the hall. Another bell rang. Another teacher—a short, dumpy man with glasses—stepped into the hallway to close his classroom door. He spotted me.

"You're late again, Amsterdam," he barked at me. "Come on, come on."

I hurried into the classroom. I hoped this class would be something I could handle. Like maybe an English class where you read comic books.

No such luck.

It was an English class, all right.

But we weren't reading comic books. We were reading a book called *Anna Karenina*.

First of all, this book is about ten thousand pages long. Second, everybody else had read it, and I hadn't. Third, even if I tried to read it, I

138

wouldn't understand what was going on in a million years.

"Since you were the last one to class, Amsterdam," the teacher said, "you'll be the first to read. Start on page forty-seven."

I sat down at a desk and fumbled around. "Um, sir"—I didn't know the guy's name— "um—I don't have the book with me."

"No, of course you don't," the teacher sighed. "Robertson, would you please lend Amsterdam your book?"

Robertson turned out to be the girl sitting next to me. What was with this teacher, anyway? Calling everybody by their last names.

The girl passed her book to me. "Thanks, Robertson," I said. She scowled at me.

I guess she didn't like being called Robertson. But I didn't know her first name. I'd never seen her before in my life.

"Page forty-seven, Amsterdam," the teacher repeated.

I opened the book to page forty-seven. I scanned the page and took a deep breath.

That page was covered with big words. Hard words. Words I didn't know.

And then long Russian names.

I'm about to make a big fool of myself, I realized.

Just take it one sentence at a time, I told myself.

The trouble was, those sentences were long. One sentence took up the whole page!

"Are you going to read or aren't you?" the teacher demanded.

I took a deep breath and read the first sentence.

"'The young Princess Kitty Shcherb— Sherba—Sherbet—'"

Robertson sniggered.

"*Shcherbatskaya,*" the teacher corrected. "Not *Sherbet.* We've been over all these names, Amsterdam. You should know them by now."

Shcherbatskaya? Even after the teacher had pronounced it for me, I couldn't say it. We never had words like that on our seventh-grade spelling tests.

"Robertson, take over for Amsterdam," the teacher commanded.

Robertson took her book back from me and started reading out loud. I tried to follow the story. It was something about people going to balls and some guys wanting to marry Princess Kitty. Girl stuff. I yawned.

"Bored, Amsterdam?" the teacher asked. "Maybe I can wake you up a bit. Why don't you tell us what this passage means?"

"Means?" I echoed. "You mean, what does it mean?"

"That's what I said."

I tried to stall for time. When would this stupid class be over, anyway?

"Um—mean? What does it mean," I murmured to myself, as if I were thinking really hard. "Like, what is the meaning of it? Wow, that's a tough one—"

All the other kids turned in their seats and stared at me.

The teacher tapped his foot. "We're waiting."

What could I do? I had no idea what was going on. I went for the foolproof escape.

"I have to go to the bathroom," I said.

Everybody laughed except the teacher. He rolled his eyes.

"Go ahead," he said. "And stop by the principal's office on your way back."

"What?"

"You heard me," the teacher said. "You've got a date with the principal. Now get out of my class."

I jumped up and ran out of the room. Man! High school teachers were mean!

Even though I was being punished, I was glad to get out of there.

I never thought I'd say this, ever. But I wanted to go back to junior high! I wished everything would go back to normal.

I wandered through the hall, looking for the principal's office. I found a door with a frosted-glass window. Letters on the window said, MRS MCNAB, PRINCIPAL.

Should I go in? I wondered. Why should I? She's only going to yell at me.

I was about to turn around and leave. But someone was coming towards me down the hall.

Someone I didn't want to see.

"There you are, you little creep!" It was the big guy from this morning. "I'm going to pound your face into the ground!"

Gulp.

Suddenly the principal's office didn't seem so scary. This guy—whoever he was—would never hurt me in the principal's office.

"You'll be needing plastic surgery when I'm finished with you!" the guy yelled.

I opened the principal's door and slipped inside.

A big woman with steely grey hair sat behind a desk, writing something.

"Yes?" she said. "What is it?"

I paused to catch my breath. Why was I there again?

Oh, yeah. English class.

"My English teacher sent me," I explained. "I guess I'm in trouble."

"Sit down, Matt." She offered me a chair. She seemed kind of nice. She didn't raise her voice. "What's the problem?"

"There's been some kind of mistake," I began.

"I don't belong here. I'm not supposed to be in high school!"

She frowned. "What on earth are you talking about?"

"I'm twelve years old!" I cried. "I'm a seventh grader! I can't do this high school work. I'm supposed to be in junior high!"

She looked confused. She reached out and pressed the back of her hand to my forehead.

She's checking to see if I have a fever, I realized. I must sound like a maniac.

She spoke slowly and clearly. "Matt, you're in eleventh grade. Not seventh grade. Can you understand me?"

"I know I *look* like an eleventh grader," I said. "I can't do the work! Just now, in English class? They were reading a big, fat book called Anna something. I couldn't read the first sentence!"

"Calm down, Matt." She stood up and went to a file cabinet. "You *can* do the work. I'll prove it to you."

She pulled out a file and opened it. I stared at it. It was a school record, with grades and comments.

My name was written at the top of the chart. And there were my grades, for seventh grade, eighth grade, ninth grade, tenth grade, and the first half of eleventh.

"You see?" Mrs McNab said. "You can do the work. You've got mostly B's, every year."

There were even a few A's.

"But—but I haven't *done* this yet," I protested. What was going on? How did I end up so far in the future? What happened to all those years?

"Mrs McNab, you don't understand," I insisted. "Yesterday, I was twelve. Today I woke up—and I was sixteen! I mean, my body was sixteen. But my mind is still twelve!"

"Yes, I know," Mrs McNab replied.

"Yes, I know you read a lot of science fiction," Mrs McNab said. "But you don't expect me to believe that silly story—do you?"

Mrs McNab folded her arms and sighed. I could tell she was losing patience with me.

"You have gym class next, don't you," she said.

"What?"

"This is all some kind of joke, right?" She glanced at my schedule, stapled to the file.

"I knew it," she muttered. "You *do* have gym next. And you're trying to get out of it."

"No! I'm telling the truth!"

"You're going to that gym class, young man," she said. "It starts in five minutes."

I stared at her. My feet felt glued to the floor. I should have known she wouldn't believe me.

"Are you going?" she asked gruffly. "Or do I have to take you to the gym myself?"

"I'm going, I'm going!" I backed out of the office and ran down the hall. Mrs McNab stuck her head out of the door and called, "No running in the halls!"

Pam and Greg always said that high school was bad, I thought as I trotted to the gym. But this is a nightmare!

Tweet! The gym teacher blew his whistle. "Volleyball! Line up to pick teams."

The gym teacher was a stocky guy with a black toupee. He chose a couple of team captains, and they started picking teams.

Don't pick me. Don't pick me, I silently prayed.

One of the captains, a blonde girl named Lisa, picked me.

We lined up at the volleyball nets. The other team served. The ball flew at me like a bullet.

"I got it! I got it!" I cried.

I reached up to hit the ball back.

Klonk! It knocked me on the head.

"Ow!" I rubbed my sore head. I'd forgotten— my head was much higher now than it used to be.

"Wake up, Matt!" Lisa yelled.

I had a feeling I wasn't going to be very good at volleyball.

The ball came flying at us again. "Get it, Matt!" someone called.

I reached up higher this time. But I tripped over my giant feet—and fell—*oof!*—on top of the guy standing next to me.

"Watch it, man!" the guy shouted. "Get off me!" Then he clutched his elbow. "Ow! I've hurt my elbow!"

The teacher blew his whistle and hurried over to the guy. "You'd better go to the nurse," he said.

The guy hobbled out of the gym.

"Way to go, Matt," Lisa said sarcastically. "Try to do something right this time, okay?"

I turned red with embarrassment. I knew I looked like a jerk. But I wasn't used to being so tall! And having such big feet and hands. I didn't know how to control them.

I got through a few rounds without messing up. Actually, the ball didn't come near me. So I didn't have the chance to mess up. Then Lisa said, "Your serve, Matt."

I knew this was coming. I'd been watching everybody else serve so I'd know what to do.

This time I won't mess up, I vowed. I'm going to serve this ball and get a point for my team. Then they won't be angry at me for making us lose.

I tossed the ball in the air. I punched it as hard as I could with my fist, trying to get it over the net.

WHAM! I hit that ball harder than I'd ever hit anything. It whizzed through the air so fast, you could hardly see it.

SMACK!

148

"Ow!"

Lisa doubled over, clutching the side of her head.

"Why did you have to hit it so hard?" Lisa cried, rubbing her head.

The teacher looked her over. "You'll have a nasty bruise there," he said. "You'd better go to the nurse too."

Lisa glared at me and stumbled away.

The teacher gave me a funny look. "What's the matter, kid?" he asked. "Don't know your own strength? Or just out to get your class-mates, one by one?"

"I—I didn't do it on purpose," I stuttered. "I swear I didn't!"

"Hit the showers, kid," the teacher said.

I hung my head as I dragged myself to the locker room.

This day can't get any worse, I thought. There's no way.

Still, why take chances?

It was lunchtime. I had half a day of school to go.

But I wasn't going to stick around.

I didn't know where to go or what to do. I only knew I couldn't stay in that school.

High school was horrible. If I ever got back to my normal life, I'd remember to skip this part.

I left the gym and raced out of the school

building as fast as I could. Down the hall. Out the door.

I glanced back. Was that big guy chasing me? Did the principal see me sneak out?

No sign of anyone. Coast clear.

Then—*oof!*

Oh, no. Not again!

I bumped into someone. I bounced backwards and landed with a thud on the ground.

Ow! What happened?

A girl sat sprawled on the pavement. Books were scattered around her.

I helped her up. "Are you okay?" I asked.

She nodded.

"I'm really sorry," I said. "I've been doing that all day."

"That's all right." The girl smiled. "I'm not hurt."

She wasn't a high school girl—she looked about my age. I mean, the age I thought I was. Which was twelve.

She was pretty, with long, thick blonde hair in a ponytail. Her blue eyes sparkled at me.

She bent down to pick up her stuff.

"I'll help you," I offered. I reached down to pick up a book.

CLONK! My head bumped into hers.

"I did it again!" I cried. I was getting sick of this.

"Don't worry about it," the girl said. She picked up the rest of the books.

"My name is Lacie," she told me.

"I'm Matt."

"What's the matter, Matt?" she asked. "Why are you in such a hurry?"

What could I tell her? That my whole life had turned inside out?

Then the school door burst open. Mrs McNab stepped outside.

"I've got to get out of here," I replied. "I've got to get home. See you."

I ran down the street before Mrs McNab could spot me.

I collapsed on the couch. It had been a terrible day. At least I'd made it home before that big guy beat me up.

But what was I going to do tomorrow?

I watched TV until Pam and Greg came home from school.

Pam and Greg. I'd forgotten all about them.

They were little kids now. And they seemed to expect me to take care of them.

"Make us a snack! Make us a snack!" Pam chanted.

"Make your own snack," I snapped back.

"I'm telling Mummy!" Pam cried. "You're

supposed to make us a snack! And I'm hungry!"

I remembered the excuse Pam and Greg had always used to get out of doing stuff for me.

"I've got homework to do," I said.

Oh, yeah, I realized.

I probably really *do* have homework to do.

High school homework.

It's going to be impossible for me.

But if I don't do it, I'll be in trouble tomorrow.

In more ways than one, I thought, remembering that big guy. What did I ever do to him, anyway?

When it was time for bed, I headed to my old room. But Pam was sleeping in there.

So I went back to the guest room. I climbed into bed.

What am I going to do? I worried as I let my eyes close.

I don't know what's happening.

I can't do anything right.

Is this what my life is going to be like—for ever?

I opened my eyes. Sunlight poured in through the window. It was morning.

Oh, great, I thought. Time for another fabulous day of high school.

I shut my eyes again. I can't face it, I thought. Maybe if I stay in bed, all my problems will go away.

"Matt! Time to get up!" Mum called.

I sighed. Mum would never let me stay home from school. There was no way out.

"Matt!" she shouted again.

Her voice sounds funny, I thought. Higher than usual.

Maybe she's not so tired for once.

I dragged myself out of bed. I set my feet on the floor.

Wait a minute.

My feet.

I stared at them. They looked different. I mean, they looked the same.

They weren't big any more. I had my old feet back!

I looked at my hands. I wiggled my fingers.

It was me! I was my old self again!

I ran into the bathroom to check the mirror. I had to make sure.

I flipped on the light.

There I was—a puny little twelve-year-old!

I hopped up and down. "Yippee! I'm twelve! I'm twelve!"

All my problems were solved! I didn't have to go to high school!

I didn't have to face that big bully!

The nightmare was over!

Everything was okay now. I was even looking forward to seeing Pam and Greg and Biggie as their crabby old selves again.

"Matt! You're going to be late!" Mum shouted.

Does she have a cold or something? I wondered as I ran downstairs. She really did sound different.

I practically skipped into the kitchen. "I'll have cereal today, Mum—"

I stopped.

Two people sat at the kitchen table. A man and a woman.

I'd never seen them before.

"I've made you some toast, Matt," the woman said.

"Where's my mother?" I asked. "Where are Pam and Greg?"

The man and woman stared blankly at me.

"Feeling a little off today, son?" the man said.

Son?

The woman stood up and bustled around the kitchen. "Drink your juice, honey. Your dad will drop you off at school today."

My dad?

"I don't have a dad!" I insisted. "My father has been dead since I was a baby!"

The man shook his head and bit into a piece of toast. "They told me he'd get weird at this age. But I didn't know *how* weird."

"Where are they?" I demanded. "What did you do with my family?"

"I'm not in the mood for jokes today, Matt," the man said. "Now let's get moving."

A cat crept into the kitchen. It rubbed against my legs.

"What's this cat doing here?" I asked. "Where's Biggie?"

"Who's Biggie? What are you talking about?" the woman said.

I was starting to get scared. My heart was pounding. My legs felt weak.

I sank into a chair and gulped my juice. "Are you saying that—you're my parents?"

The woman kissed me on the head. "I'm your mother. This is your father. That's your cat. Period."

"I have no brothers or sisters?"

The woman raised an eyebrow and glanced at the man. "Brothers and sisters? No, darling."

I cringed. My real mother would never call me "darling".

"I know you want a brother," the woman went on. "But you really wouldn't like it. You're just not good at sharing."

I couldn't stand this any longer.

"Okay, stop right there," I demanded. "Stop fooling around. I want to know right now—why is this happening to me?"

My "parents" exchanged looks. Then they turned back to me.

"I want to know who you are!" I cried, trembling all over. "Where is my real family? I want answers—now!"

The man stood up and grabbed me by the arm. "Get in the car, son," he commanded.

"No!" I screamed.

"Joke is over. Now get in the car."

I had no choice. I followed him to a car—a shiny new one, not my real mother's old piece of junk. I climbed in.

The woman ran outside. "Don't forget your books!" she called. She pushed a backpack through the open window at me. Then she kissed me again.

"Ugh!" I cringed. "Stop it!" I didn't know her well enough to let her kiss me.

The man started the car and pulled out of the driveway. The woman waved. "Have a good day at school!"

They're serious, I realized. They really think they're my parents.

I shuddered.

What was happening to me?

One day I'm a normal twelve-year-old. The next day I'm suddenly sixteen.

Then the next day I'm twelve again—except I live in a completely different family!

I stared out the window as "Dad" drove. We passed through a neighbourhood I'd never seen before.

"Where are we going?" I asked in a tiny voice.

"I'm taking you to school. What did you think—we were going to the circus?" the man replied.

"This isn't the way to school," I said.

The man just snorted and shook his head. He didn't believe me.

He pulled up in front of a junior high school— but not mine. I'd never seen this place before.

"Okay, son. Have a nice day." The man reached across me and opened the car door.

What could I do? I climbed out of the car.

"Dad" drove off.

Now what? I thought. I'm twelve again—but I'm at a totally different school.

Am I awake?

I kicked myself in the shin to test it. Ow! That hurt.

I figured that meant I was awake.

Kids poured into the school building. I followed them in. I didn't know what else to do.

Ahead of me I saw a girl with a long, thick blonde ponytail. She turned around and smiled at me.

She looked familiar. Where had I seen her before?

"Hi," I said to her.

"Hi," she said back. Her blue eyes sparkled at me.

"I'm Matt." I was still racking my brains trying to figure out where I'd met her before.

"I'm Lacie."

Lacie! Of course. I'd crashed into her the day before—outside Horrible High.

I started to say, "I met you yesterday—remember?" But I stopped.

Did she recognize me? I couldn't tell. But why should she? I looked completely different from the day before. How could she guess that the twelve-year-old kid standing next to her was also the clumsy teenager from yesterday?

"What's your first class?" she asked me. "I've got lunch."

"Lunch? But it's eight-thirty in the morning!"

"You're new here, aren't you?" she said.

I nodded.

"This stupid school is so crowded, they can't fit everyone into the cafeteria at lunchtime," she explained. "So I've got lunch now."

"I've got lunch too," I lied. Or maybe it wasn't a lie—What did I know? I had no idea what was going on any more. School was beginning to seem like a lot more trouble than it was worth.

I followed her to the cafeteria. They really were serving lunch there. The powerful smell of Brussels sprouts stank up the air. I gagged.

"It's too early in the morning for Brussels sprouts," I noted.

"Let's eat out in the playground," Lacie suggested. "It's a nice day."

We slipped out of the cafeteria and settled under a tree. Lacie sipped a carton of chocolate milk. I rummaged through my backpack for some lunch. I figured my new "mum" must've packed me something.

She had all right. Corned beef and ketchup on white bread. A little plastic bag full of carrot sticks. Vanilla pudding for dessert.

Everything I hate.

Lacie held out a chocolate cupcake. "Want this? I can't face it this early in the morning."

"Thanks." I took the cupcake.

Lacie seemed like a really nice person. She

161

was the nicest person I'd met since my life became a nightmare. She was the *only* nice person I'd met since then.

Maybe she would understand. I really wanted to talk to somebody. I felt so alone.

"Do I look familiar to you?" I asked her.

She studied my face.

"You do look kind of familiar," she said. "I'm sure I've seen you around school . . ."

"That's not what I mean." I decided to tell her what had happened to me. I knew it would sound weird to her. But I had to tell somebody.

I started slowly. "Were you walking past the high school yesterday?"

"Yes. I walk past it every day on my way home."

"Did someone bump into you yesterday? A teenager? In front of the high school?"

She started to answer. But something caught her eye. I followed her gaze to the school door.

Two guys were walking towards us. They were tough-looking guys in black jeans and black T-shirts. One wore a blue bandanna around his head. The other had ripped the sleeves of his T-shirt to show off his beefy arms.

They had to be at least sixteen or seventeen. What were they doing here?

They headed straight for us.

My heart began to pound. Something told me to be afraid of them.

Maybe it was the nasty looks on their faces.

"Who are those guys?" I asked.

Lacie didn't answer. She didn't have time.

One of the guys in black pointed at me.

"There he is!" he shouted.

"Get him!"

The two guys ran straight for me.

Who were they? I didn't know.

But I didn't stop to think. I jumped to my feet and ran as fast as I could.

I glanced back. Were they chasing me?

"Stop him!" one of them shouted.

Lacie stepped in front of them, blocking their path.

"Thanks, Lacie," I whispered. I hurried out of the playground. I raced through the strange neighbourhood, trying to remember how to get home.

A few blocks from school I stopped to catch my breath.

No sign of the two guys. No sign of Lacie, either.

I hope she's all right, I thought. They didn't seem to want to hurt her.

They wanted to hurt *me*.

But why?

The day before, a bully had said he wanted to get me after school.

But today, in my new, weird world, I hadn't seen him. Neither of the guys in black was that bully.

Just two *new* bullies.

I've got to get help, I realized.

I don't know what's happening. But it's all too much for me. And it's too frightening. I hardly know who I am.

I drifted through the streets until I finally found my way home. "Mum" and "Dad" were out. The front door was locked. I climbed in through the kitchen window.

My real mother was gone. My brother and sister and even my dog were gone.

But there must be someone else I know, I thought. Somebody, somewhere, who can help me.

Maybe my real mum went somewhere else. Maybe she's visiting relatives or something.

I decided to try Aunt Margaret and Uncle Andy. I dialled Aunt Margaret's number.

A man answered the phone.

"Uncle Andy!" I cried. "It's me, Matt!"

The voice said, "Who is this?"

"Matt!" I repeated. "Your nephew!"

"I don't know any Matt," the man said gruffly. "You must have dialled the wrong number."

"No—Uncle Andy, wait!" I shouted.

"My name isn't Andy," the man snarled. He hung up.

I stared at the phone, stunned. The man didn't sound like Uncle Andy at all.

I guess I *did* dial wrong, I thought. I tried the number again.

"Hello?" It was the same man again.

This time I tried a new approach. "Is Andy Amsterdam there, please?"

"You again! There's no Andy here, kid," the man said. "Wrong number."

He slammed the phone in my ear.

I tried not to panic. But my hands were shaking.

I dialled information. "What listing, please?" the operator asked.

"Andrew Amsterdam," I said.

"Checking," said the operator.

A minute later she said, "I'm sorry. We have no listing under that name."

"Maybe if I spell it for you," I insisted. "A-m-s—"

"I've already checked, sir. There's no one listed under that name."

"Could you try Margaret Amsterdam, then?"

"There's no one named Amsterdam listed at all, sir."

My heart started racing as I hung up. This can't be happening, I thought. There must be somebody I know, somewhere!

I won't give up. I'll try my cousin Chris.

I called Chris's number. Someone else answered.

It was as if Chris didn't exist. Or Uncle Andy, or my mother, or anybody I knew.

How could my whole family disappear?

The only person I knew was Lacie. But I couldn't call her.

I didn't know her last name.

The front door opened. The woman who called herself my mother bustled in, carrying shopping bags.

"Matt, darling! What are you doing home in the middle of the day?"

"None of your beeswax," I snapped.

"Matt! Don't be so rude!" she scolded.

I shouldn't have been rude to her, I guess. But what difference did it make? She wasn't my real mother, anyway.

My real mother had disappeared off the face of the earth. I shuddered. I realized I was totally alone in the world.

I didn't know anyone—not even my parents!

"Bedtime, honey," my fake mother chirped.

I'd been sitting in front of the TV all evening. Just staring, not even really watching it.

Maybe I should stop thinking of these people as my fake parents, I realized. They're real enough now. I might be stuck with them for ever.

I'll find out in the morning, I thought as I trudged upstairs. My old room was a sewing room now. I went back to the guest room to sleep.

"Good night, darling." "Mum" kissed me good night. Why did she have to keep kissing me?

She turned out the light and said, "See you in the morning."

The morning. I dreaded the morning.

So far, each morning was weirder than the last. I was scared to go to sleep.

What would I wake up to?

It would be great if these fake parents of mine were gone. But who would take their place?

Maybe I'd wake up and the whole world would be gone!

I struggled to stay awake. Please, I prayed. Please let everything be normal again. I'd even be glad to have Greg and Pam back, if everything could only be normal . . .

I must have fallen asleep. The next thing I knew, I opened my eyes—and it was morning.

I lay perfectly still for a minute. Had anything changed?

I heard noises in the house. There were definitely other people here.

A *lot* of other people.

My heart started pounding. Oh, no, I thought. What am I in for this time?

I heard someone playing an accordion. That was a pretty sure sign my old family wasn't back.

But first things first. How old was I today?

I held my hands up in front of my face. They looked a little on the small side.

I got up and went to the bathroom, trying not to panic. I was really getting sick of this routine.

The mirror seemed higher than usual. I stared at my face.

I wasn't twelve any more, that was for sure. I looked about eight.

Eight, I thought, sighing.

That's third grade. Well, at least I'll be able to do the maths.

Suddenly, I felt a sharp pain in my back.

Ow! Claws! Tiny claws digging into my back! The claws dug deeper.

I screamed!

Something jumped on my back!

A tiny, hairy face appeared in the mirror. Some kind of animal was standing on my shoulders!

"Get it off! Get it off!" I shrieked.

"Eeee! Eeee!" the animal screeched.

I ran into the hallway—and almost crashed into a huge man.

"Get this thing off me!" I cried.

The man plucked the animal off my shoulder. He laughed loud and deep, like an evil Santa Claus.

"What's wrong with you, Matt?" he boomed. "Scared of Pansy all of a sudden?"

Pansy? The man cuddled the animal in his arms. It was a monkey.

The man roughed up my hair. "Get dressed, boy. We've got a rehearsal this morning."

Rehearsal? What was that supposed to mean?

I stared at the man. He was huge, with a

round stomach, glossy black hair, and a long moustache.

The weirdest part was what he wore: a bright red costume with gold trim and a gold belt.

Oh, no! I thought, my heart sinking. This can't be . . . my father?

From downstairs a woman's voice screamed, "Grub!"

The man handed me a pile of clothes. "Put your costume on," he said. "Then come on down to breakfast—son."

I knew it. He *was* my father. For today, at least. My "family" kept getting worse every day.

"GRU-U-U-U-B!" the woman downstairs yelled again.

I guess that's Mum, I thought miserably. She sounds like a real sweetheart.

Kids came pouring out of the other bedrooms. It seemed like there were dozens of them, all different ages. But I counted, and there were only six.

I tried to get all the new facts straight. I was eight years old. I had six brothers and sisters and a pet monkey. I hadn't seen my mother yet, but my father was a total wacko.

And I've got to wear some kind of freaky costume, I thought, holding up the clothes the man had given me. It was a tight blue outfit, like a leotard. The bottom part was blue with white stripes. The top had white stars.

What was that supposed to be? And what kind of rehearsal did I have?

Was I in a play or something?

I pulled on the costume. It fit me like a second skin. I felt like a total jerk.

Then I went downstairs for breakfast.

The kitchen was a madhouse. The other kids laughed and shouted and threw food. Pansy hopped around on the table, stealing bits of bacon.

A tall, thin woman piled pancakes on plates. She wore a long, purple, sequinned gown. A silver crown perched on top of her head.

My new mum.

"Hurry up and eat, Matt—before it's all gone!" she shouted.

I grabbed a plate and started eating. I had to keep swatting Pansy away.

"Doesn't Matt look cute in his little superhero suit?" a girl teased. She had to be one of my older sisters.

"Cute as a button," a boy said sarcastically. He looked about two years older than me. He grabbed my cheek and pinched it—hard. Too hard. "Cute little Matt," he sneered. "Big-shot star of the circus."

The circus! I dropped my fork. Chills rippled down my back. Was I in the circus?

The dopey costumes. The monkey. It all made sense now.

I dropped my head into my hands. Matthew Amsterdam, circus boy. I almost wanted to cry.

I had the feeling my brother was jealous. As if *he* wanted to be the star of the stupid circus.

And he could be, for all I cared. *I* sure didn't want to be the star of any circus.

"Leave Matt alone or he'll get stage fright again," the mother scolded.

I studied the rest of the family. Everyone was dressed in bright costumes. I was part of a circus family.

The pancakes sank to the pit of my stomach. I'd never liked the circus. Even when I was little, I hated it.

But now the circus was my life—and I was the star. Oh, goody.

"Rehearsal time!" the father cried. He put a black top hat on his head and cracked a whip on the stairs. "Let's roll!"

We left our plates on the table and piled into a beat-up old van. Mum drove at about ninety miles an hour.

My brothers and sisters fought the whole way. One little girl kept pinching me. Another one punched me.

"Cut it out!" I snapped. Why couldn't I wake up in a world with *nice* brothers and sisters?

The van chugged into a fairground and stopped in front of a big circus tent.

"Everybody out!" Dad ordered.

174

I jostled with my brothers and sisters to get out of the van. Then I followed them into the tent.

It was kind of awesome inside the tent. Other acts were already there, practising. I saw a man on a high wire way up near the top of the tent. An elephant stood up on its hind legs and danced. Clowns rode around in dopey little cars, honking their horns.

I wonder what *my* act is? I thought. Two of my sisters scurried up a ladder and started practising a trapeze routine.

I watched them, terrified. The trapeze! There was *no way* they could get me up there. *No way*.

Please don't make me do a trapeze act, I prayed.

"Come on, Matt," Dad said. "Let's get to work."

Not the trapeze. Not the trapeze, I prayed.

Dad led me away from the trapeze ladder. I began to relax. Whatever I had to do, it couldn't be worse than swinging around on a trapeze. Right?

Wrong.

Dad led me to the back of the tent. I followed him through a maze of animal cages.

Dad strode up to one of the cages and opened the door.

"All right, son," he bellowed. "Get in."

My jaw dropped. I couldn't believe my ears.

"G-g-g-get in?" I stuttered. "But—there's a *lion* in that cage!"

The lion opened his huge jaws and roared. I backed away, shivering.

"Are you going to walk in?" Dad prodded me with the end of his whip. "Or do I have to push you?"

I didn't move. I couldn't.

So Dad pushed me into the lion's cage—and shut the door.

I backed up against the cage wall. The cold steel
bars pressed into my back. My legs were trembling so hard, I thought I would fall on my face.

The lion stared at me. He sniffed the air.

I've heard that animals can smell fear. This
lion got a noseful.

My "father"—the lion tamer—stood beside
me in the cage.

"We're trying a new trick today, Matt," he
said. "You're going to ride the lion."

He might as well have punched me in the
stomach. I was going to ride the lion?

Yeah. Right.

Some father this guy is, I thought. Feeding
his own son to a lion.

The lion stood up. I kept my eyes on him. My
whole body shook with fear.

R-O-O-O-A-A-A-R!

The lion's breath blew in my face like a hot
wind. My hair stood on end.

The lion stepped towards us. Dad cracked his whip. "Ha!" he shouted.

The lion stepped back, licking his chops.

"Go on, boy," Dad boomed at me. "Climb on Hercules's back. Then slide up to his shoulders. I'll crack the whip to make him walk around the cage."

I couldn't say a word. I just stared at the man in total disbelief.

"Why are you looking at me like that? You're not afraid of Hercules, are you?"

"A-afraid?" I stammered. "Afraid" wasn't the word. "*Petrified*", maybe. Terrified, horrified, frozen with fear. But afraid? Nah.

He cracked his whip again. "No son of mine is a coward!" he shouted. "You get on that lion's back—NOW!"

Then he leaned down and whispered, "Just watch that he doesn't bite you. Remember your poor brother Tom. He's still trying to learn how to write left-handed."

He cracked the whip again—right at my feet.

I wasn't going to ride the lion. No way.

And I couldn't stay in that cage another second.

Dad cracked his whip at me again. I jumped. "Noooo!" I shrieked.

I tugged the cage door open. I ran out of that cage so fast, Dad hardly knew what happened.

I raced out of the tent. My brain screamed, "Hide! Find a hiding place—quick!"

I spotted a couple of trailers in the parking lot.

I darted behind one—and bumped right into Lacie.

"You again!" I gasped. It was weird how she kept popping up.

"I've got to hide," I told her. "I'm in trouble!"

"What's wrong, Matt?" she asked.

"I'm about to become lion food!" I cried. "Help me!"

Lacie yanked on the trailer door. It was locked.

"Oh, no!" I groaned. "Look!"

I pointed past the trailer. Two guys were running towards us.

I'd seen them before. The two guys in black.

They were coming after me!

I ran. There was no place to go, no place to hide—except back inside the tent.

I burst through the tent flap. I tried to catch my breath while my eyes adjusted to the dark.

I heard one of the guys in black shout, "In there! He went inside the tent!"

I stumbled through the darkness, searching for a place to hide.

"Get him!" The boys were inside the tent now.

I ran blindly—right back into the lion's cage.

I slammed the cage door shut. The guys in black gripped the steel bars and shook them.

"You won't get away!" one shouted.

My "dad", the lion tamer, was gone. I was alone in the cage—with Hercules.

"Easy, boy. Easy . . ." I murmured as I inched my way along the side of the cage. The lion stood in the centre, eyeing me.

The two guys rattled the cage door again. It swung open. They stepped inside, glaring at me.

"You can't escape that easily," one of them warned.

The lion growled at them. "It's just an old circus lion," one guy said doubtfully. "He won't hurt us."

But I could tell they weren't as sure as they sounded.

Hercules growled again, louder this time. The two guys stopped.

I inched further around the cage wall.

I had to put that lion between me and the guys in black. It was my only chance.

Carefully, one of the guys stepped forward. The lion roared at him.

He stepped back.

The lion's eyes darted from the guys to me and back. I knew he was trying to decide who would make the tastier meal.

"You'd better get out of here," I warned. "Hercules hasn't been fed yet."

The guys watched Hercules warily.

"He won't attack me," I bluffed. "I'm his master. But if I tell him to, he'll go right for your throats!"

The guys glanced at each other. One of them said, "He's lying."

The other guy didn't look so sure.

"I'm not lying," I insisted. "Get out of here right now—or I'll turn him on you!"

One guy made a move for the cage door. The other guy grabbed his arm and pulled him back. "Don't be chicken," he snapped.

"Get them, Hercules!" I shouted. "Get them!"

Hercules let out his fiercest roar yet—and pounced.

The guys in black scurried out of the cage. They slammed the door as Hercules tried to bound out.

"You won't get away!" one guy yelled through the bars. "We'll be back!"

"Why do you want me?" I screamed after them. "What did I do? What did I do?"

Hercules didn't really want to eat anybody. He just wanted to get out of the cage.

He didn't try to stop me as I slipped out. I sneaked away to hide in the van until circus practice was over.

"Where were you all day?" Dad grumbled when he found me. Everyone else piled into the van, and we drove home.

"I felt sick," I complained. "I had to lie down."

"You're going to learn that trick tomorrow, Matt," Dad insisted. "You *won't* get out of it again."

I just yawned. I figured tomorrow would never come. At least not for my circus family.

Tomorrow would bring some new horror. Or maybe for once something good would happen.

I went to bed early that night. I didn't like being an eight-year-old in a circus family. I couldn't wait for it to be over.

My circus brothers were climbing the walls in

my old room. I'd never get any sleep in there. So I crept off to sleep in the guest room again.

But I had trouble falling asleep. I couldn't stop wondering what the next day would bring. It's hard to relax when you don't know what kind of world you'll wake up to in the morning.

I tried counting sheep, but that never works for me. So I tried to think of all the good things that could happen when I woke up.

I could wake up as a major league baseball player. I could be the greatest pitcher in the history of baseball.

Or I could be a very, very rich kid who gets everything he wants.

Or I could be a space explorer five hundred years in the future.

Why didn't anything like *that* ever happen to me?

Most of all, I wished I could wake up and find my family again. My *real* family. They drove me crazy. But at least I was used to them. I even missed them, a little bit.

Okay, a *lot*.

At last, just before dawn, I fell asleep.

It was still very early when I woke up. I gazed around the room. Everything seemed a little blurry.

Who am I now? I wondered. The room looked

normal. I didn't hear any noise, so I knew the circus family was gone.

Might as well get it over with, I decided. I jumped out of bed. I felt a little shaky on my legs.

I walked slowly into the bathroom. I looked in the mirror.

No. Oh, no.

This was the worst one yet. The worst ever. The worst *possible*!

I was an old man!

"No!" I screamed. I couldn't take it any more. I ran back to bed as fast as my rickety old legs would carry me.

I got under the covers and closed my eyes. I was going right back to sleep. I wasn't about to spend the whole day as an old man. Not when I'm really only twelve.

I quickly dozed off. When I woke up, I knew right away I had changed. I wasn't an old man any more.

I felt a surge of energy. Power. I felt strong.

Maybe I'm a baseball player after all, I thought hopefully.

I rubbed my eyes. That's when I caught a glimpse of my hand.

It—it was *green*. My skin was green. And instead of fingers, I had claws!

I swallowed hard. I tried to shake away my panic.

What had happened to me this time?

I didn't waste a second finding out. I lumbered to the bathroom mirror.

When I saw my face, I let out a roar of horror and disgust.

I had become a monster. A hideous, gross monster.

I tried to scream. I tried to shout, "This can't be happening to me!"

But all that came out was a terrifying snarl.

No! I thought, in a total panic. I felt like tearing my horrible skin off. I was a hideous monster—and I couldn't even talk!

I was big—almost seven feet tall—and powerful. My skin was a scaly green with black stripes, like a lizard. I oozed slime all over.

My head looked like a dinosaur's, with warts all over it. Three spiky horns stuck out of the top of my head, between four pointy ears.

My hands and feet had sharp claws. My toenails clicked on the bathroom floor when I walked.

I was one ugly, ugly dude.

I wished I'd stayed an old man. Each time I woke up, my life got worse! When was this ever going to end? How could I make it stop?

I thought about Lacie. She seemed to pop up no matter where I went.

And she had tried to help me escape from those guys in black, I remembered. She wants to help me.

I've got to find her, I decided. I know she's out there somewhere.

She's my only chance.

I staggered through the house in my monster body. The house was empty. At least I didn't have a family to deal with. A family full of monsters would have been a *real* nightmare!

I had to be grateful for the little things. Especially when I had green skin and spikes growing out of my head.

I lumbered out the door and down the street. I tried to shout, "Lacie! Lacie, where are you!"

But my mouth couldn't make the words. All that came out was a booming, terrifying roar.

A car driving down the street stopped suddenly. The driver gaped at me through the windscreen.

"Don't be afraid!" I cried. But that's not what came out. Another roar ripped through the air.

The man screamed and backed his car down the street at full speed. He crashed into a car.

I went over to see if anyone was hurt. A woman and her kid were in the other car.

They must have been all right. Because as soon as they saw me, they all jumped out of their cars and ran away, screaming their heads off.

My giant lizard feet carried me to the centre of town. I smashed through bushes, kicked dustbins over. People screamed in terror as soon as they saw me.

Lacie, I thought. I've got to find Lacie.

I tried to keep this thought in my head. But I was getting hungry. Very, very hungry.

Normally I like peanut butter and jelly for a snack. But that day I had a strong craving for metal. A nice, big, crunchy hunk of metal.

The town was in a panic. People raced around, shrieking as if it were the end of the world.

But I wasn't going to hurt anybody. All I wanted was a little snack.

I stepped in front of a tasty-looking compact car. The driver slammed on the brakes.

R-O-O-A-A-R-R! I beat my chest with my powerful monster arms.

The driver cowered in the car. I reached out and snatched off a windscreen wiper. Just for a taste.

Mmmmm. Rubbery goodness.

The man flung the car door open. "No!" he cried. "Don't hurt me! L-leave me alone!"

He ran away to hide somewhere. It was nice of him to leave me his car.

I ripped the door off the car. I pulled the handle off and stuffed it into my mouth.

Delicious. Nice cool chrome.

Then I took a big bite out of the door. Chomp,

chomp. My teeth were huge and sharp as a razor—they had no trouble chewing the metal. Yum—leather upholstery for extra flavour. I finished off the door and reached in to rip out a bucket seat.

Bits of yellow foam rubber spewed out of my mouth as I ate. The leather was yummy. But the foam padding was kind of dry. It was like air-popped popcorn with no butter. Bleh.

I was tearing out the steering wheel when I heard sirens.

Uh-oh.

I saw that a mob had gathered around me. People pointed at me.

"He's eating a car!" someone screeched.

Well, duh, I thought. What do you expect a monster to eat—Rice Krispies?

The sirens came closer. Police cars were pulling up all around me.

"Clear the way," came a voice over a loudspeaker. "Stand back. Clear the way."

I'd better get out of here, I decided. I dropped the steering wheel I was nibbling and began to run. People screamed and scattered out of the way.

"Stop him! Get the monster!"

The squeal of police sirens ripped through the air. If they caught me, I knew they'd try to lock me up—or worse.

I had to get out of there. I had to hide.

I stumbled through the crowds. I headed for the edge of town.

Then I spotted her. Lacie. Mobs of people were running away from me. She was the only one running *towards* me.

I snarled, trying to call Lacie. She grabbed me by my slimy arm and pulled me out of the crowd.

She led me down an alley. We lost the mob. I wanted to ask her where we were going. But I knew the words wouldn't come. I was afraid a roar might scare her.

We ran and ran. We didn't stop running until we reached the woods at the edge of town. Lacie pulled me into the woods, deeper and deeper.

She's hiding me, I thought gratefully. I wished I could thank her.

I followed Lacie down a narrow path. Then the path ended. We pushed our way through the brush.

At last we came to a small house. It was well hidden by trees and vines. You could hardly see it, even when you stood right in front of it.

A hideout, I thought. How did Lacie find this place?

I wondered if there was anything good to eat inside the house. I was getting hungry again.

A couple of bicycles would taste good right now, I thought.

Lacie opened the door of the house. She beckoned me to come inside.

I went in. Two people stepped out of the shadows.

No, oh, no.

Not them.

But it *was* them.

The guys in black.

One of them spoke.

"Thank you for bringing him to us," he said. "You did your job well."

RRRROOOOOOAAAAARRRR!

I thrashed my arms. I was furious!

Lacie had betrayed me!

I had to get out of there—fast.

I leapt for the door—but they dropped a net over me.

They yanked on the net—and I tripped.

I fell with a heavy thud. The two guys closed the net over me.

I roared and thrashed with all my might. But I couldn't get out. They tied the net tightly around me.

"Get me out of here!" I wanted to scream. I slashed at the net with my claws. I bit it with my teeth. But it was made of some kind of strange material. I couldn't break the strings.

I snarled and kicked for a long time. But no matter what I did, I was still trapped. At last I got tired. I lay on my back on the floor.

Lacie and the two guys in black stared down at me, perfectly calm.

I wished I could talk. I couldn't stop myself from trying.

"How could you do this to me?" I tried to ask Lacie. "I thought you were my friend!"

Nothing but snarls and growls came out of me. Lacie stared down at me. She couldn't understand what I said.

The guys in black just folded their arms across their chests and sneered at me.

"Who are you?" I wanted to ask them. "What do you want? What is happening to me?"

No one answered me. One of the guys, the taller one, said, "All right. Let's lock him up in the back."

I roared again. I struggled as the three of them dragged my big, slimy body across the floor. They pushed me into a small room at the back of the house. They locked me inside.

The room was dark. There was one small window with metal bars on it.

I could eat those bars, I realized. If I could reach them.

But I was stuck on the floor. I couldn't move inside the tight net.

I lay still for a long time, waiting for something to happen. But no one returned to the room. I couldn't hear what they were doing in the other rooms.

Through the window I saw the light fading. Night was coming.

I knew there was nothing I could do but fall asleep—fall asleep—and hope I'd wake up human again.

I woke up groggy. My stomach hurt.

Man, I thought. What did I eat yesterday? It feels as if I've got a big lump of metal in my stomach!

Then I remembered. I *did* have metal in my stomach.

Oh, yeah. I had snacked on a compact car. Mum always told me not to eat too many snacks.

I've got to remember not to do *that* again.

I sat up. I checked myself out.

Whew. I was human again.

What a relief.

The net lay open around me. Someone had cut it off while I was sleeping.

But who was I now?

My arms and legs were skinny. My feet were floppy and too big for my legs.

But they weren't *that* big. Not monster big.

I was a boy again. But not my usual twelve-year-old self.

I figured I was about fourteen.

Well, I thought, it's better than being a monster.

A *lot* better.

But I'm still in that house in the woods, I realized. I'm still a prisoner.

Those two guys in black had finally caught me.

What did they want? What were they going to do to me?

I stood up and tried the door. Locked.

I glanced at the window. There was no way I could break through those bars.

I was trapped.

I heard a key in the lock. They were coming!

I cowered in a corner of the room.

The door swung open. Lacie and the two guys stepped in.

"Matt?" Lacie said. She spotted me in the corner. She took a step towards me.

"What are you going to do to me?" I asked.

It was good to hear words coming out of my mouth again. Instead of just roars.

"Let me go!" I cried.

The guys in black shook their heads.

"We can't do that," the shorter guy said. "We can't let you go."

They stepped closer. They clenched their hands into fists.

"No!" I shouted. "Stay away from me!"

The tall guy slammed the door shut. Then they moved in on me.

They walked steadily towards me. I glanced frantically around the room for a way to escape.

The guys blocked my path to the door. There was no way out.

"We're not going to hurt you, Matt," Lacie said gently. "We want to help you. Really."

The guys took another step towards me. I shrank back. They sure didn't *look* like they wanted to help me.

"Don't be afraid, Matt," Lacie said. "We need to talk to you."

She sat down in front of me. She was trying to show me I shouldn't be afraid.

But the two guys stood guard on either side of her.

"Tell me what's happening to me," I demanded.

Lacie cleared her throat. "You're trapped in a Reality Warp," she explained.

As if I'd know what she was talking about.

"Oh, of course. A Reality Warp," I cracked. "I knew *something* weird was going on."

"Cut the comedy," the shorter guy snarled. "This is no joke. You're causing us a lot of trouble."

Lacie hushed him. "Quiet, Wayne. I'll handle this."

She turned back to me and asked in her soft voice, "You don't know what a Reality Warp is, do you?"

"No," I replied. "But I know I don't like it."

"When you fell asleep in your guest room, you fell into a hole in reality," she said.

The more she told me, the less it made sense. "There's a hole in reality—in the guest room?"

She nodded. "You fell asleep in one reality, and woke up in another. You've been stuck in that hole ever since. Now, whenever you go to sleep, you change what is real and what isn't real."

"Well, make it stop!" I demanded.

"I'll stop *you*," the tall guy threatened.

"Bruce—please," Lacie snapped.

"What does all this have to do with you, anyway?" I asked.

"You're breaking the law, Matt," she said. "Every time you change, you break the laws of reality."

"I'm not doing it on purpose!" I protested. "I've

never even heard of the laws of reality! I'm innocent!"

Lacie tried to soothe me. "I know you're not doing it on purpose. But it doesn't matter. It's happening. When you change bodies, you change what is real and what isn't real for a lot of people. If you keep changing, you'll throw the whole world into confusion."

"You don't understand!" I cried. "I want to stop it! I'll do anything to stop it! I just want to be normal again!"

"Don't worry," Wayne murmured. "We're going to stop it."

"We're the Reality Police," Lacie told me. "Our job is to keep reality under control. We've been trying to keep up with you, Matt. It hasn't been easy, with all the changes you've made."

"But why?" I asked. "What are you going to do?"

"We had to capture you," Lacie said. "We can't allow you to break the reality laws."

I thought quickly. "It's the guest room, right? This all happened because I slept in the guest room?"

"Well—"

"I'll never sleep in the guest room again!" I promised. "I don't mind if I don't change back to my old self. This skinny fourteen-year-old body is not so bad."

Lacie shook her head. "It's too late for that,

Matt. You're trapped in the hole. It doesn't matter whether you sleep in the guest room or not. Every time you go to sleep—and wake up—you change reality. No matter where you are."

"You mean—I can never fall asleep again?"

"That's not quite it." Lacie glanced at the two guys. Then she trained her blue eyes on me.

"I'm sorry, Matt. I really am. You seem like a nice guy."

An icy chill slithered down my spine. "What—what are you talking about?"

She patted my hand. "We have no choice, Matt. We have to put you to sleep—for ever."

I stared at her in horror.

"You—you can't do that!" I stammered.

"Oh, yes, we can," Wayne said.

"And we will," Bruce added.

"No!" I shouted. I leapt to my feet and made a dive for the door. But Bruce and Wayne were ready for me. They grabbed me and held my arms behind my back.

"You're not going anywhere, kid," Wayne said.

"Let go of me!" I screamed.

I struggled and squirmed. But I wasn't a gigantic monster any more. I was a scrawny kid—no match for Bruce and Wayne. Even Lacie probably could have beaten me up if she wanted to.

The guys tossed me against the back wall of the room.

"We'll be back later," Lacie promised. "Try not to worry about it too much, Matt. It won't hurt."

They left the room. I heard the key turn in the lock.

I was trapped again.

I searched the room for a way to escape. It was completely empty—no furniture at all, not even a chair. Just four bare walls, a locked door, and a small window with metal bars.

I opened the window and rattled the bars. I hoped they might be loose or something. But they didn't budge.

It was like being in jail. Jailed by the Reality Police.

I put my ear to the door, listening. I could hear Lacie, Bruce and Wayne talking in the other room.

"He'll have to drink the sleeping potion," Wayne said. "Make sure he drinks the whole cup—or he might wake up."

"But what if he spits it out?" Lacie asked. "What if he doesn't swallow it?"

"I'll make him swallow it," Bruce vowed.

Yikes! I couldn't listen any more. I frantically paced the room.

They were going to feed me a sleeping potion! To make me sleep for ever!

I'd been in trouble before. My day in high school had seemed scary at the time. Being a monster was scary too. But, now—now I was really done for.

I've got to find a way out of this mess! I told myself. But how? How?

Then it dawned on me. How did I get out of trouble before?

I fell asleep. And the problem went away.

True, I always woke up with new, worse problems. But nothing could be worse than this!

Maybe, I hoped, if I fall asleep, I'll wake up somewhere else. And that's how I can escape!

I paced some more.

The only trouble was—how could I fall asleep? I was so terrified!

I knew I had to try, anyway. So I lay down on the floor. There was no bed, no pillow, no blanket. Daylight streamed in through the barred window.

Falling asleep wasn't going to be easy.

You can do it, I told myself. I remembered how my mum—my real mum—used to say I could fall asleep in a hurricane. I'm a good sleeper, it's true.

I missed my mum. It seemed like I hadn't seen her in a long, long time.

If only there were some way I could bring her back, I thought as I closed my eyes.

When I was very little, she used to sing me to sleep. I remembered the lullaby she sang. It was all about pretty ponies. . .

I hummed the song to myself. Before I knew it, I'd drifted off to sleep.

I opened my eyes. I rubbed them. Had I fallen asleep?

Yes.

Where was I?

I looked up. Plain ceiling.

I looked around. Bare walls.

A door.

A window. With bars on it.

"No!" I cried, furious. "No!"

I was still in the same room, in the same house in the woods.

I was still a prisoner.

My plan didn't work.

Now what could I do?

"Nooooooo!"

I was so angry, so frustrated, so scared, I jumped up and down in a rage.

My plan hadn't worked. I had no more ideas. I didn't know what to do.

Now I knew for sure there was no escape for me.

I was doomed.

I heard Lacie and the two guys in the other room. They were getting the sleeping potion ready.

They'd put me to sleep for ever. I'd never see my mother, or Greg, or Pam, again.

How could they do this to me? It wasn't fair!

I didn't do anything wrong. Not on purpose, anyway!

Thinking about all this made me angrier and angrier. I screamed, "NOOOOOOOOOOO!"

And it sounded strange to me.

I screamed again, not so loud this time.

"Nooooo!"

I thought I was saying, "No." But that's not what I heard.

I heard a squeak.

"No!" I said again.

"*Eee!*" I heard.

It was my voice. But it wasn't a human voice.

I looked at myself. I'd forgotten to do that. I'd been so terrified to find myself still trapped—I didn't think that maybe I had changed.

But I *had* changed.

I was small. About twenty centimetres tall.

I had tiny little paws. Grey fur. A big bushy tail.

I was a squirrel!

My eyes went to the windows. I could easily squeeze through the bars now.

I didn't waste a second. I scampered up the wall and wriggled through the bars.

I was free!

Yippee! I did a little squirrel somersault to celebrate.

Then I ran through the woods as fast as I could. I found the path to town.

I scurried through town on my little squirrel feet. It seemed to take a long time. Short distances felt longer to me.

All was quiet in town. Normal. No sign that a monster had ever stomped through, chomping on cars.

I guess that reality disappeared, I thought.

This is the new reality. I'm a squirrel.

But at least I'm an *awake* squirrel. It's better than being a boy who has to sleep for ever.

I sniffed the air. I had an amazing sense of smell. I thought I could smell my house from the middle of town.

I raced across the street. But I forgot what my mother always told me.

Look both ways before you cross.

A car peeled around the corner. The driver couldn't see me.

Huge black tyres bore down on me. I tried to scurry out of the way.

But I didn't have time.

209

I shut my eyes. Is this how I'll end up? I wondered.

As roadkill?

SCREECH!

The driver slammed on the brakes. The car squealed to a stop.

Then everything was quiet.

I opened my eyes. One tyre came so close, it touched my ear.

I zipped out from under the tyre and across the street. The car sped away.

I reached the pavement. A dog stood guard in a yard. He barked at me.

Whoops! I dodged him and ran up a tree. The dog chased me, barking furiously.

I camped out in that tree until the dog got bored. His owner called him. He trotted away.

I sneaked out of the tree and dashed through the yard.

The rest of the way home I dodged cars, bikes, people, dogs, cats . . .

Then, at last, I found myself staring up at my house. It was nothing special, my house. Just a white square house with peeling paint.

But it looked beautiful to me.

I had a new plan. An idea that would stop this craziness once and for all.

I hoped.

My whole problem had started when I slept in the guest room, I knew. That's where the hole in reality was—Lacie had said so.

But ever since then—ever since I'd slept in the guest room—I hadn't slept in my own room. Not once.

Something always stopped me. Either someone else was sleeping there, or it was being used for something else.

My own room was where I slept when my life was normal. My tiny old room. I never thought I'd miss it.

I decided I *had* to sleep in my old room again. Maybe that way, I could turn everything back to normal. The way it used to be.

I knew it sounded stupid. But it was worth a try.

And, anyway, I didn't have any other ideas.

I scampered up the rain gutter to the second floor. I peeked through my old bedroom window.

There it was! My old room. With my bed in it and everything!

But the window was closed. I tried to push it with my tiny squirrel paws. No luck.

I checked the other windows in the house. They were all shut.

There had to be another way to get in. Maybe I could sneak through the door somehow.

Was anyone home? I peered through the living room window.

Mum! And Pam and Greg!

They were back!

I got so excited, I hopped up and down. I chirruped and chittered.

Then Biggie waddled into the room.

Oh, yeah. I'd forgotten about Biggie. I wasn't too glad to see him right then.

Biggie loved to chase squirrels.

He saw me right away and started barking.

Pam looked up. She smiled and pointed at me.

Yes! I thought. Come and get me, Pam. Open the window and let me in!

She gently opened the window. "Here, little squirrel," she cooed. "You're so cute!"

I hesitated. I wanted to go inside. But Biggie was barking like crazy.

"Put Biggie in the basement!" Pam told Greg. "He's scaring the squirrel."

She was being nicer to me as a squirrel than she ever was to her little brother. But I let that slide for now.

Greg led Biggie to the basement and shut the door.

"Come on, squirrel," Pam chirped. "It's safe now."

I hopped into the house.

"Look!" Pam cried. "He wants to come in! It's almost like he's tame!"

"Don't let him in here!" Mum warned. "Those animals have rabies! Or bugs, at the very least."

I tried not to listen. It's hard to hear your own mother insult you that way.

I focused on getting upstairs. If I could only get up to my room and fall asleep, just for a few minutes. . .

"He's getting away!" Greg shouted. "Catch him!"

Pam pounced at me. I skittered away.

"If that squirrel gets lost in this house, Pamela," Mum warned, "you're going to be in big, big trouble."

"I'll catch him," Pam promised.

Not if I can help it, I silently vowed.

Pam cut me off at the stairs. I darted into the kitchen.

Pam followed. She closed the kitchen door behind her.

I was trapped.

"Here, little squirrel," she called. "Here, boy."

I twitched my tail. I searched the room for a way out.

Pam inched her way towards me. She was trying not to scare me away.

I scurried under the table. She dived for me. Missed.

But when I scampered away, she cornered me.

And snatched me up.

I never knew she was so speedy.

She grabbed me by the neck and held my feet together. "I've got him!" she shouted.

Greg threw open the kitchen door. Mum stood behind him.

"Take him outside—quick!" Mum ordered.

"Can't I keep him, Mum?" Pam begged. "He'd be such a cute pet!"

I shuddered. Me, as Pam's pet! What a nightmare!

But it might be my best chance to get back to my room.

"No!" Mum insisted. "You absolutely cannot keep him. Put him outside—now."

Pam's mouth drooped. "Okay, Mum," she said sadly. "Whatever you say."

She carried me out of the kitchen. "Mum is so mean," she said loudly so Mum could hear her. "All I wanted to do was pet you and cuddle you for a while. What's wrong with that?"

A lot, I thought. Pam was the last person I wanted petting and cuddling me. Except for Greg.

She opened the front door. "Bye, you cute little squirrel," she said.

Then she slammed the door shut.

But she didn't let me go. She held me tightly in her arms.

Then she slipped upstairs to her room.

215

"Don't worry, squirrel," she whispered. "I won't keep you very long. Just a little while."

She pulled something out from under her bed. Her old hamster cage.

She opened the door of the cage. She shoved me inside.

"No!" I protested. But all I could do was squeak.

She locked the latch.

I was a prisoner again!

Now what am I going to do? I thought frantically. I'm stuck in this stupid cage. I can't talk.

How will I ever get to my old room?

Another bad thought came to me.

If I fell asleep in this tiny hamster cage—what would happen when I woke up?

Pam's big face loomed over the cage. "Are you hungry, squirrely-kins? I'll go and get you some nuts or something."

She left the room for a minute. I paced the cage, thinking hard. The next thing I knew, I was running on the hamster wheel.

Stop it! I told myself. I made myself get off the wheel. I didn't want to get used to being a rodent.

"Here you go, squirrel." Pam had returned to the room with a handful of nuts. She opened the door to the cage and sprinkled the nuts inside.

"Yum yum!" she squealed.

Oh, brother.

I ate the nuts. I was very hungry after all

my adventures. But I would have enjoyed them more if Pam hadn't watched me the whole time.

The phone rang. A moment later I heard Greg call, "Pam! Telephone!"

"Excellent!" Pam cried. She jumped up and ran out of the room.

Like a moron, I sat there gobbling nuts. It took me five minutes to notice that Pam had left the cage door unlatched.

"Yes!" I squeaked. For once I was glad that Pam was no genius.

I pushed the door open with my paws. I crept toward the bedroom door, listening for footsteps.

The coast was clear. Now was my chance!

I dashed out the door. Down the hall. To my room.

The door was shut. I threw my tiny squirrel body against it, trying to open it.

No way. It was closed tight.

Rats!

I heard footsteps down the hall. Pam was coming back!

I knew I had to get out of there before Pam put me back in that cage.

Or before my mother swatted me with a broom.

I scurried down the steps and into the living room.

Was the window still open? Yes.

I ran behind the couch, along the wall, under a chair . . .

Then I leaped up to the windowsill and out into the yard.

I climbed a tree and curled up on a branch to rest.

I couldn't get into my old room as a squirrel. There was only one thing I could do.

I had to go to sleep again. And this time, I'd better wake up as a human.

, Because I had to get to my old room. If I didn't, I'd be in trouble.

Big trouble.

The Reality Police were on my trail. It was only a matter of time before they'd find me.

If they did, nothing could save me.

CRASH! THUD!

OOF!

I landed hard on the ground. What a way to wake up.

Who was I this time?

What a relief. I was a twelve-year-old boy again.

But I still wasn't my old self.

I was a very, very chubby boy. A real blimp. No wonder the tree branch didn't hold me.

But that didn't matter. I was a human again. I could talk.

And maybe now I could get to my old room at last.

I marched straight up to the front door and tried the knob.

Locked.

So I knocked.

I had no idea who would answer. I hoped it wasn't a monster family.

The door opened.

"Mum!" I cried. I was so glad to see her. "Mum—it's me! Matt!"

Mum stared at me. "Who are you?" she asked.

"Matt! Matt, Mum! Your son!"

She squinted at me. "Matt? I don't know anyone called Matt," she said.

"Sure you do, Mum! Don't you remember me? Remember that lullaby you used to sing to me when I was a baby?"

She narrowed her eyes suspiciously.

Greg and Pam appeared behind her. "Who is it, Mum?" Pam asked.

"Greg!" I shouted. "Pam! It's me, Matt! I'm back!"

"Who is this kid?" Greg asked.

"I don't know him," Pam said.

Oh, no, I thought. Please don't let this be happening. I'm so close. . .

"I need to sleep in my old room," I begged. "Please, Mum. Let me go upstairs and sleep in my room. It's a matter of life and death!"

"I don't know you," Mum said. "And I don't know any Matt. You have the wrong house."

"This kid is some kind of wacko," Greg said.

"Mum! Wait!" I cried.

Mum slammed the door in my face.

I turned around and started down the drive. What do I do now? I wondered.

Then I stopped. I glanced down the block.

Three people were running towards me. The last three people I wanted to see.

Lacie, Bruce and Wayne.

The Reality Police! They'd found me!

"There he is!" Lacie pointed at me. The three of them started to run.

"Get him!"

I turned and ran. It wasn't easy. I couldn't run very fast.

Why did I have to wake up chubby this time?

I did have one advantage. I knew the neighbourhood inside out—and they didn't. I ran across the yard to the next-door neighbour's house.

I glanced back. The Reality Police were gaining on me. They were half a block away.

I disappeared behind the neighbour's house. Then I sneaked back around to my house.

At the back of the garage is a line of thick shrubs. I threw myself behind the shrubs and held my breath.

A few minutes later, three pairs of feet hurried past me.

"Where'd he go?" I heard Lacie ask.

"He must've gone the other way," Wayne said. "Come on!"

They ran off.

Whew. I could breathe again. I let out a whoosh of air.

Safe for now. But I knew the Reality Police would find me again.

I had to get back to my room. But there was no way Mum would let me in. She thought I was a total nutcase.

There was only one thing to do. I had to break into the house.

I'd wait until nighttime. Till everyone was asleep.

Then I'd find an open window somewhere— or break one if I had to.

I'd sneak into my room and sleep there. I hoped I wouldn't find someone else sleeping there.

In the meantime, I had to wait for night. I stayed hidden behind the shrubs. I lay as still as I could.

And I struggled to stay awake. I didn't want to fall asleep again.

If I fell asleep, who knew what I'd be? I might never get to my room.

The hours dripped slowly by. At last night came. The neighbourhood got quiet.

I pulled myself out of the shrubs. My legs and arms ached from hiding.

I looked at the house. Everyone had gone to bed, except for Mum. Her bedroom light was still on.

I waited until it went off. I waited another half hour to give her time to fall sound asleep.

Then I crept around to the front of the house. My room was on the second floor.

I knew Mum had locked all the doors. I knew she'd locked all the first-floor windows. She did that every night.

I had to climb to the second floor and sneak in through my window. It was the only way.

I had to climb up the tree that grew by my window. Then reach out and grab the rain gutter.

Then set myself down on the narrow ledge outside my window. I'd have to cling to the gutter for balance.

If I could make it to the ledge, I might be able to open the window and crawl in.

That was the plan, anyway. The more I thought about it, the more stupid it sounded.

Better not think about it, then, I decided. Just do it.

I stood up on my toes, stretching towards the lowest branch of the tree. It was just out of reach. I'd have to jump.

I bent my knees and sprang up. My fingertips grazed the branch, but I couldn't get a grip on it.

If only I weren't so chubby! I could barely get off the ground.

I won't give up, I vowed. If this doesn't work, I'm doomed.

So I took a deep breath. I gathered all my strength.

I crouched down. I sprang up as high as I could.

Yes! I grabbed the branch!

I hung there for a second, wriggling. I kicked my legs. They were so heavy!

I twisted around and walked my legs up the tree trunk. With a grunt of effort, I hoisted myself on to the branch.

Whew.

The rest of the tree was pretty easy. I climbed up until I reached the branch just outside my window.

I grabbed a branch over my head as I stood up. I could just reach the rain gutter. I sure hoped it would hold.

I grasped the gutter. I tried to put my foot on the window ledge.

I missed.

I was hanging by my fingertips from the gutter!

I looked down. The ground seemed far away.

I squeezed my lips shut to keep myself from screaming.

I panted, hanging there. I had to get my foot on that ledge—or I'd fall.

I wriggled to the left, trying to get closer to the ledge.

CRACK!

What was that?

CRACK!

The gutter! It wasn't going to hold!

CRACK!

I felt myself sink. The gutter was about to give way.

I mustered all my strength. Clinging to the gutter, I stretched one leg out as far as it would go. My toes touched the window ledge.

I set one foot down. Then the other.

I made it!

I crouched on the ledge. I clung to the gutter with one hand, for balance.

I didn't move. I tried to catch my breath. The night was cool. But I felt drops of sweat trickle down my face. I wiped them away with my free hand.

I peered through the window. My room was dark. Was anybody in there?

I couldn't tell.

The window was shut.

Please don't let it be locked, I prayed.

If I couldn't get in, I'd be stuck up on the ledge. I'd have no way to get down.

Unless I fell down, of course.

I carefully tried the window. It slid up. It wasn't locked!

I pushed it open. Then I crawled into the room. I tumbled on to the floor.

I froze. Did anyone hear me?

No sounds. Everyone was still asleep.

I pulled myself to my feet. There was my bed! My old bed! And it was empty!

I was so happy, I wanted to jump up and shout. But I didn't.

I'll save the celebration for tomorrow, I decided. If my plan works.

I took off my shoes and crawled into bed. I sighed. Clean sheets.

It felt good to be back. Everything was almost normal.

I was sleeping in my own bed. Mum and Pam and Greg were all asleep in their rooms.

Okay, I didn't look like myself. I didn't have my old body back yet.

And my family didn't recognize me. If they saw me now, they'd think I was a burglar. Or a maniac.

I pushed those things out of my mind. I wanted to think about the morning.

What will happen tomorrow? I wondered sleepily.

Who will I be when I wake up? Will my life be normal again?

Or will I find Lacie and those two guys standing over me, ready to pounce?

There was only one way to find out. I closed my eyes and drifted off to sleep.

I felt something warm on my face. Sunlight.

I opened my eyes. Where was I?

I glanced around. I was in a small, cramped, messy room full of junk.

My old room!

My heart skipped a beat. Had my plan worked? Was I back to normal?

I couldn't wait to find out. I threw off the covers and jumped out of bed. I hurried to the mirror on the back of my bedroom door.

I saw a skinny, blond, twelve-year-old boy. Yes! I was back!

I was me again!

"Woo-hoo!" I cried.

Biggie nosed the door open and waddled into the room. He growled at me. He barked.

"Biggie!" I cried happily. I bent down and hugged him. He snapped at me.

Good old Biggie.

"Matt!" I heard Mum's voice call from the kitchen. My *real* mum's voice.

"Matt! Leave Biggie alone! Stop teasing him!"

"I'm not teasing him!" I yelled back. She always blames me for everything.

But I didn't care! I was so glad to be back!

I scrambled downstairs for breakfast.

There they sat. Mum. Pam. Greg. Just the way I'd left them.

"The geek enters the kitchen for his morning feeding," Greg spoke into his tape recorder. "What does a geek eat? Let's watch and find out."

"Greg!" I sang. I threw my arms around his neck and hugged him.

"Hey!" He swatted me away. "Get off me, geek!"

"And Pam!" I gave her a big hug too.

"What's your problem, pea-brain?" she snapped. "I know—you got kidnapped by aliens last night! Am I right? And they brainwashed you!"

I ignored her jokes. I patted the top of her Brillo pad hair.

"Cut it out!" she whined.

I gave my mum the biggest hug of all.

"Thanks, honey." She patted me on the back. At least *she* was on my side, once in a while.

"Get some cereal, Matt," she said. "I'm running late."

I sighed happily and fixed myself some cereal.

Everything was back to normal. No one even noticed I'd been gone.

I'm never going into that stupid guest room again, I vowed. Never. I'm going to stay in my little room from now on—no matter how cramped it gets.

Thwack! Something stung me on the back of the neck.

I whirled around. Greg grinned at me. He held a straw in one hand.

He spoke into the tape recorder. "What happens if you shoot a paper wad at the geek? How does he respond?"

"I bet he cries like a baby," Pam said.

I shrugged and went back to my cereal. "You can't bother me," I said. "I'm too happy."

Pam and Greg exchanged glances. Pam twirled one finger at the side of her head. It was the international signal for "He's nuts".

"Something has happened to the geek," Greg announced.

"Yeah," Pam agreed. "The geek has changed."

School was so much fun that day. It was great to be in seventh grade again. So much easier than high school.

We played soccer in gym. I even scored a goal.

But on my way to my last class, I saw something that made my heart stop.

A girl walking down the hall. About my age. Long, thick blonde hair in a ponytail.

Oh, no.

Lacie!

I froze. What should I do?

Were the Reality Police still after me? I had fixed everything! They didn't need to put me to sleep any more!

I've got to get out of here, I decided. I got ready to run.

Then the girl turned around. She grinned at me.

It wasn't Lacie. Just some girl with long blonde hair.

I took a deep breath. I need to relax, I thought.

It's over now. It was all a bad dream. Sort of.

The girl walked away. I went to my last class. No sign of Lacie, Bruce, or Wayne anywhere.

I whistled all the way home, thinking about how easy my homework was going to be.

I walked into the house. "Hi, Matt!" Mum called.

"Mum?" I was surprised to see her. She was usually at work when I got home. "What are you doing home so early?"

She smiled at me. "I took the day off," she explained. "I had a few things to do around the house."

"Oh." I shrugged and turned on the TV.

Mum switched it off. "Matt—aren't you curious?"

"Curious? About what?"

"About what I've been doing all day?"

I glanced around the living room. Everything looked the same.

"I don't know," I said. "What have you been doing?"

She smiled again. She looked excited about something.

"Have you forgotten?" she said. "It's your birthday this week!"

Actually, I *had* forgotten. So much weird stuff had been going on.

When you're running for your life, you don't think much about your birthday.

"I have a special surprise for you," Mum said. "Come upstairs and I'll show you."

I followed her upstairs. I started getting excited. What could the surprise be?

It wasn't like Mum to make such a big deal about my birthday. The surprise must be something really great, I decided.

She stopped in front of my bedroom door.

"Is the surprise in my room?" I asked.

"Look." She pushed open the door.

I peered inside. My room was filled with boxes. Big boxes from floor to ceiling.

Wow!

"Are all those presents for me?" I asked.

Mum laughed. "Presents? All those boxes? Of course not!" She cracked up.

I knew it had to be too good to be true.

"Well—what's the surprise, then?" I asked.

"Matt," she began, "I've been thinking about what you said the other day. And I decided you were right. Your room is too small for you. So I've turned it into a box room."

"You—you what?"

"That's right." She walked across the hall.

She threw open the guest room door. "Ta-da!"

No. Oh, no.

It can't be. Not that.

"Happy Birthday, Matt!" Mum shouted. "Welcome to your new room!"

"Uh . . . uh . . . uh . . ." I couldn't say a word.

My bed, my dresser, all my posters and books—they were all set up in the guest room.

"Matt? What's the matter?" Mum cried. "This is what you said you wanted!"

My mouth fell open. I started to scream.

Goosebumps

The Blob That Ate Everyone

"I used to believe in monsters," Alex said. She pushed her glasses up on her nose. Her nose twitched. With her pink face and round cheeks, she looked like a tall, blonde bunny rabbit.

"When I was little, I thought that a monster lived in my sock drawer," Alex told me. "You won't believe this, Zackie. But I never opened that drawer. I used to wear my trainers without socks. Sometimes I tried to go barefoot to first school. I was too scared to open that drawer. I knew the sock monster would bite my hand off!"

She laughed. Alex has the strangest laugh. It sounds more like a whistle than a laugh. "*Wheeeeeeh! Wheeeeeeh!*"

She shook her head, and her blonde ponytail shook with her. "Now that I'm twelve, I'm a lot smarter," she said. "Now I know that there is no such thing as monsters."

That's what Alex said to me *two seconds* before we were attacked by the monster.

*   *   *

It was the Easter holidays, and Alex and I were out collecting things. That's what we do when we can't think of anything better.

Sometimes we collect weird-looking weeds. Sometimes we collect insects. Or odd-shaped leaves.

Once, we collected stones that looked like famous people. That didn't last long. We couldn't find that many.

If you get the idea that Norwood Village is a boring town . . . you're right!

I mean, it *was* boring until the monster attacked.

Alex Iarocci lives next door to me. And she is my best friend.

Adam Levin, who lives across town, is my best friend too. I think a person should have a *lot* of best friends!

I'm not sure why Alex has a boy's name. I think it's short for Alexandria. But she won't tell me.

She complains about her name all the time. It gives her a lot of trouble.

Last year at school, Alex was assigned to a boys' gym class. And she gets mail addressed to *Mr* Alex Iarocci.

Sometimes people have trouble with my name too. Zackie Beauchamp. My last name is pronounced BEECH-am. But no one ever knows how to say it.

Why am I going on about names like this?

I think I know why.

You see, when the Blob Monster attacked, I was so scared, I forgot my own name!

Alex and I had decided to collect worms. Only purple worms—no brown ones.

That made the search more interesting.

It had rained the day before, a long, steady, spring rain. Our backyards were still soft and spongy.

The worms were coming up for air. They poked through the wet grass. And wriggled on to the driveway.

We were both crouched down, searching for purple ones—when I heard a loud, squishy sound behind me.

I spun around quickly.

And gasped when I saw the monster. "Alex— look!"

She turned too. And a whistling sound escaped her mouth. *"Wheeeeh!"* Only *this* time, she wasn't laughing.

I dropped the worm I had been carrying and took a *biiig* step back.

"It—it looks like a giant human heart!" Alex cried.

She was right.

The monster made another loud *squish* as it bounced over the grass towards us. It bounced like a giant beach ball, taller than Alex and me. Nearly as tall as the garage!

It was pink and wet. And throbbing.

BRUM BRRUUM BRUMMM. It pulsed like a heart.

It had two tiny black eyes. The eyes glowed and stared straight ahead.

On top of the pink blob, I thought I saw curled-up snakes. But as I stared in horror, I realized they weren't snakes. They were thick, purple veins—arteries tied together in a knot.

BRRUUUM BRUM BRUMM.

The monster throbbed and bounced.

"Ohhhhhh!" I groaned as I saw the sticky trail of white slime it left behind on the grass.

Alex and I were taking giant steps—backwards. We didn't want to turn our backs on the ugly thing.

"Unh unh unh!" Terrified groans escaped my throat. My heart had to be pounding at a hundred miles an hour!

I took another step back. Then another.

And as I backed away, I saw a crack open up in the creature's middle.

At first I thought the pink blob was cracking apart.

But as the crack grew wider, I realized I was staring at its mouth.

The mouth opened wider. Wider.

Wide enough to swallow a human!

And then a fat purple tongue plopped out. The tongue made a wet *SPLAT* as it hit the grass.

"*Ohhhh.*" I groaned again. My stomach lurched. I nearly lost my lunch.

The end of the tongue was shaped like a shovel. A fat, sticky, purple shovel.

To shovel people into the gaping mouth?

Thick, white slime poured from the monster's mouth. "It—it's *drooling*!" I choked out.

"Run!" Alex cried.

I turned—and tripped on the edge of the driveway.

I landed hard on my elbows and knees.

And looked back—in time to see the drooling, pink mouth open wider as the tongue wrapped around me . . . pulling me, pulling me in.

Alex stared at me, her mouth open wide. "Zackie, that is *awesome!*" she declared.

Adam scratched his curly, black hair and made a face. "You call that scary?" He rolled his eyes. "That's about as scary as *Goldilocks and the Three Bears.*"

I held the pages of my story in one hand. I rolled them up and took a swing at Adam with them.

He laughed and ducked out of my reach.

"That is an awesome story!" Alex repeated. "What do you call it?"

"'Adventure of the Blob Monster'," I told her.

"Oh, wow," Adam exclaimed sarcastically. "Did you think that up all by yourself?"

Alex gave Adam a hard shove that sent him tumbling on to the sofa. "Give Zackie a break," she muttered.

The three of us were hanging out in Adam's house. We were squeezed into what his parents call the rec room.

The room is so small. Only a sofa and a TV fit.

It was the Easter holidays, and we were hanging out because we didn't know what else to do. The night before, I had stayed up till midnight, working on my scary story about the Blob Monster.

I want to be a writer when I grow up. I write scary stories all the time. Then I read them to Alex and Adam.

They always react in the same way. Alex always likes my stories. She thinks they're really scary. She says that my stories are so good, they give her nightmares.

Adam always says my stories aren't scary at all. He says he can write better stories with one hand tied behind his back.

But he never does.

Adam is big and red-cheeked and chubby. He looks a little like a bear. He likes to punch people and wrestle around. Just for fun. He's actually a good guy.

He just never likes my stories.

"What's wrong with this story?" I asked him.

The three of us were crammed on to the sofa now. There was nowhere else to sit.

"Stories never scare me," Adam replied. He picked an ant off the sofa arm, put it between his thumb and finger, and shot it at me.

He missed.

"I thought the story was *really* scary," Alex said. "I thought you had really good description."

"I *never* get scared by books or stories," Adam insisted. "Especially stories about stupid monsters."

"Well—what *does* scare you?" Alex demanded.

"Nothing," Adam bragged. "I don't get scared by films, either. Nothing ever scares me."

And then he opened his mouth wide in a scream of horror.

All three of us did.

We leaped off the sofa—as a terrifying *screech* rang through the room.

And a black shadow swept over the floor.

The shadow swooped by our feet, so fast I could barely see it.

I felt something brush my ankle. Something soft—and ghostlike.

"Whoooa!" Adam cried.

I heard hurried footsteps from the living room. Mr Levin—Adam's dad—burst into the doorway. With his curly black hair and bearlike, round body, Mr Levin looks a lot like Adam.

"Sorry about that!" he exclaimed. "I stepped on the cat. Did it run past here?"

We didn't answer him.

We were so stunned, we all burst out laughing.

Mr Levin frowned at us. "I don't see what's so funny," he muttered. He spotted the cat, hiding beside the sofa. He picked it up and hurried away.

The three of us dropped back on to the sofa. I was still breathing hard. And I could still feel the brush of the cat on my ankle.

"See, Zackie?" Adam cried. He slapped me hard on the back—so hard I nearly fell off the sofa. "That was a lot scarier than any story you could write."

"No way!" I insisted. "I can write a scarier story than that. The stupid cat just surprised us."

Alex pulled off her glasses and wiped the lenses on her T-shirt. "What a *screech* that cat made!" she exclaimed, shaking her head.

"I wasn't scared at all," Adam claimed. "I was just trying to scare you guys." He reached over and rubbed the palm of his hand back and forth over my head.

Don't you *hate* it when people do that?

I slugged him as hard as I could.

He only laughed.

Alex and I stayed for dinner. Mrs Levin is a great cook. We always try to be around Adam's house at dinnertime because she always invites us to stay.

It was dark by the time Alex and I started to walk home. We'd had thunderstorms the day before and most of today. The lawns glistened from the rain. The wet street reflected the glow of street lights.

I could hear the crackle of thunder somewhere far away. As Alex and I made our way along the pavement, cold rainwater dripped on us from the trees.

Adam lives on the other side of Norwood Village. But it isn't a very long walk—only about fifteen minutes.

We'd walked for about five minutes when we came to a row of little shops.

"Hey—!" I cried out when the antiques shop on the corner came into view. "It—it's been destroyed!"

"It looks as if a *bomb* hit it!" Alex exclaimed.

We stayed on the corner, staring across the street at it. Part of the roof had fallen in. All the windows were shattered. One wall had nearly caved in. The shingles on the walls and the roof had been burned black.

"Was it a fire?" I wondered, leading the way across the street.

"Lightning," a woman's voice replied.

I turned to see two young women on the pavement beside the shop. "It was struck by lightning," one of them said. "Yesterday. During the big storm. The lightning started a huge fire."

"What a mess," the other woman sighed. She pulled car keys from her pocket.

The two women disappeared around the corner, *tsk-tsking* about the shop.

Alex and I stepped up to the front.

"Ooh, it stinks," Alex groaned, holding her nose.

"It just smells burned," I replied. I glanced

down and saw that I had stepped into a deep puddle.

I jumped back.

"It's soaked everywhere," Alex murmured. "From the fire hoses, I guess."

A gust of wind made the front door bang.

"It's open!" I exclaimed.

The door had been taped shut. But the tape had broken off. A large yellow sign on the door declared in big black letters: DANGER—KEEP OUT.

"Alex—let's take a peek," I urged.

"No way! Zackie—stop!" Alex cried.

Too late. I was already inside.

I took a couple of steps into the shop and waited for my eyes to adjust to the darkness. Water dripped everywhere. An entire wall of shelves had toppled over. Broken vases, and lamps, and small statues lay scattered over the puddled floor.

"Zackie—!" Alex grabbed my shoulder "Zackie—get *out* of here!" she whispered. "This is really dangerous."

"Leave the door open," I told her. "We need the light from the street."

"But what do you want to *see*?" Her voice echoed over the *PLUNK PLUNK PLUNK* of dripping water.

She grabbed my other arm and started to tug me out. "Come on. You saw the sign. The whole building may fall in on us."

I jerked my arm away. My trainers squished as I walked. The carpet was soaked.

"I just want to look around for one second," I told Alex impatiently. "This is cool!"

"It isn't cool," she argued. "It's really stupid."

A row of ugly antique masks stared at us from one wall. The masks were tilted at odd angles. Other masks stared up from where they had fallen on the floor.

A tall wooden clock had its face burned black. Wooden duck decoys lay on their sides, burned and cracked.

A creaking sound overhead made me jump. I heard Alex gasp.

I raised my eyes to the ceiling. Part of it had fallen in. Was the rest about to collapse on top of us?

"Zackie—let's go!" Alex urged. She backed up towards the door. Her shoes squished over the soaked carpet.

The door banged shut behind us. I turned and saw the wind blow it back open.

Plink plink. Cold water dripped on to my shoulder.

"If you don't come, I'm going without you!" Alex called. "I mean it, Zackie."

"Okay, okay," I muttered. "I'm coming. I just wanted to see what happened."

"Hurry!" Alex urged. She was halfway out the door.

I turned and started to follow her.

But I stopped when something on a high shelf caught my eye.

"Hey, Alex—" I called. "Look!"

I pointed up to an old typewriter. "Wow. My dad used to have one like that when I was really little," I said.

"Zackie—I'm leaving," Alex warned.

"I *love* old typewriters!" I cried. "Look, Alex. I don't think the fire hurt it. I think it's in good condition. I just want to look it over. Okay?"

I didn't wait for her to reply.

I crossed the room. Stepped up to the shelf. Stood on tiptoe and reached for the old typewriter.

"O WWWWWWW!"

I felt a hard shock of pain. It shot through my body.

Stunned me.

Took away my breath.

Over my stunned cry, I heard the sharp *crackle* of electricity.

And I bent over—helpless—as a bright blue flame shot around my body.

Blue.

I saw only blue.

The deepest blue I'd ever seen.

I'm floating in the sky, I realized. I'm weightless. And I'm floating. Floating in the blue, blue sky.

The blue faded to white.

Was I still floating? Was I moving at all?

Was I *breathing*?

I struggled to speak. To shout. To make any kind of a sound.

The white faded quickly. To grey. Then black.

"Ohhhh," I heard myself moan.

Dark. So dark now. I was surrounded by darkness.

I blinked. Blinked again. And realized I was staring into the darkness of the ruined antique shop.

"Zackie? Zackie?"

I heard my name. Heard Alex repeating my name.

I cleared my throat. I sat up. My eyes darted around the shop.

"Zackie? Zackie? Are you okay?"

I tried to shake my dizziness away. My whole body tingled. Tingled and hummed, as if an electrical current were running through me.

"How did I get on the floor?" I asked weakly.

Alex leaned over me, one hand on my shoulder. "You got a shock," she said, squinting hard at me through her glasses. "There must be a wire down or something."

I rubbed the back of my neck. I couldn't stop the strange tingling or the steady hum in my ears.

"Wow," I murmured.

"It was a really bad shock," Alex said softly. "I—I was so scared. You were inside a blue flame. Your whole body—it turned bright blue."

"Wow," I repeated, still fighting the dizziness.

"Your hands shot up in the air," Alex continued. "And then you bent in two. And fell to the floor. I—I thought . . ." Her voice trailed off.

PLINK PLINK.

I could hear the drip of water again. The hum in my ears had faded.

I pulled myself shakily to my feet. I stretched my arms over my head, trying to stop the strange tingling.

The old typewriter caught my eye again.

"Zackie—what are you doing?" Alex cried.

255

I moved carefully to the shelf, stepping around a puddle of water on the carpet. I took a deep breath. Stretched up on tiptoe. And pulled the old typewriter down.

"Whoa—! It weighs a ton!" I cried. "It's solid metal!"

I held it in my arms and examined it. The sleek black surface caught the glow of the street light outside the door. The round keys poked up towards me.

"It's awesome!" I exclaimed. "This typewriter, Alex—it's *perfect* for writing scary stories on."

"Are you *crazy*?" Alex declared. "Zackie, I think that electric shock messed up your brain!"

"But look at it!" I insisted excitedly. "It's perfect. Perfect!"

Alex rolled her eyes. "You have a brand new computer at home," she reminded me. "And your mum gave you her old laser printer— remember?"

"I know, I know," I muttered.

"You can print eight pages a minute," Alex continued. "So what do you need a creaky old typewriter for?"

"I need it because it's perfect," I told her. "Perfect! Perfect!"

"Stop repeating that word," she snapped. "Are you sure you're feeling okay? That was a horrible shock. Maybe I should call your parents."

"No. No, I'm fine," I insisted. The typewriter

was growing heavy in my arms. "Let's just go."

Lugging the typewriter, I started to the door. But Alex blocked my path.

"You can't just *take* it!" she scolded. "It doesn't belong to you. That's stealing."

I made a face at her. "Alex, don't be stupid. Everything in this shop is wrecked. Nobody will care if I take—"

I stopped with a gasp when I heard the squish of shoes on the wet carpet.

Then I heard a cough.

I turned to Alex. Caught the fear on her face. She heard the sounds too.

"Zackie, we're not alone in here," she whispered.

Another squishy footstep. Closer.

A chill swept down my back. I nearly dropped the typewriter.

"Hide," I whispered. I didn't need to suggest it. Alex was already slipping behind a tall display shelf.

I set the typewriter down on the floor. Then I crept behind the shelf and huddled close to Alex.

I heard another cough. And then a circle of light moved across the wet carpet. The pale yellow beam of a torch.

The light slid over the floor. Then it started to climb the display case. Alex and I ducked low. The circle of light washed over our heads.

My legs were trembling. I gripped the back of the case with both hands to keep myself from falling over.

"Hello?" a voice called. A woman's voice. "Hello? Is someone in here?"

Alex turned to me. She motioned with her head.

She was silently asking if we should step out and show ourselves.

I shook my head no.

How could we explain what we were doing inside the shop? How could we explain why we were hiding?

Maybe the woman will leave, I told myself. Maybe she won't find us.

Who *is* she? I wondered. Does she own the shop?

I peered out around the bottom shelf. I could see the woman from the side. She was African-American. She had very short, dark hair. She wore a long raincoat.

She moved the torch beam along the back wall. It lit up the fallen shelf, the broken antiques.

Her footsteps slogged over the wet carpet.

"Hello?" she called. "Did someone come in here?"

I held my breath.

Please leave, I begged silently. Please don't catch us here.

The woman turned. Her light stopped on the typewriter in the middle of the floor. She kept the light steady, staring at the typewriter.

I knew what she was thinking: *How did the typewriter get on the floor?*

Slowly, she raised the light. Raised it back to the display shelf.

She stared right at us!

Could she see us hiding behind the display case?

I froze. I pretended to be a statue.

Did she see us?

No.

She muttered something to herself. The light went out.

I blinked in the sudden darkness. Her footsteps moved away.

I realized I was still holding my breath. I let it out slowly, trying not to make a sound.

Silence now. And darkness.

No footsteps. No beam of yellow light.

The front door banged shut.

Alex and I exchanged glances.

Was the woman gone? Did she leave the shop?

We didn't move.

We waited. And listened.

Silence . . .

Then Alex sneezed.

"Gotcha!" the woman cried from somewhere behind us.

A hand grabbed my shoulder. Hard.

The sleeve of the raincoat brushed my face as the woman tugged me out from behind the shelf. I nearly tripped over the typewriter. The woman held me up by one arm.

Alex stepped up beside me. Her ponytail had come undone. Her blonde hair was wild around her face. She kept swallowing hard, making dry, clicking sounds with her tongue.

I guessed she was as frightened as I was.

The woman switched her torch on. She raised it to my face, then to Alex's.

"Were you doing some late shopping?" she demanded.

"Huh?" I managed to choke out.

"The shop is closed. Couldn't you tell?" the woman snapped.

She was young and pretty. She locked her dark eyes on me.

"What are you doing in here?" she asked.

I opened my mouth to answer, but no sound came out.

"Uh ... nothing," Alex said weakly. "We weren't doing anything."

The woman narrowed her eyes at Alex. "Then why were you hiding?"

"You f-frightened us," I stammered, finally finding my voice.

"Well, you frightened me too!" the woman exclaimed. "You frightened me a lot. I was in the back room, and . . ."

"We were walking home. We saw the shop. How it was wrecked," I explained. "We just wanted to see what it looked like inside. So we came in. That's all."

The woman lowered the light to the floor. "I see," she said softly.

Her shoe made a squishing sound on the carpet. Water dripped steadily from the ceiling behind us.

"What a mess," the woman sighed. Her eyes travelled around the ruined shop. "I'm Mrs Carter. I own this shop. What's left of it."

"We—we're sorry," Alex stammered.

"You shouldn't be in here," Mrs Carter scolded. "It's very dangerous. Some of the electrical wires are down. You didn't touch anything—did you?"

"No. Not really," Alex replied.

"Well . . . just this old typewriter," I said, gazing down at it.

"I *wondered* how it got down there," Mrs Carter said. "Why did you move it?"

"I . . . like it," I told her. "It's really cool."

"Zackie writes stories," Alex told Mrs Carter. "Scary stories."

Mrs Carter let out a bitter laugh. "Well, you could certainly write a scary story about *this* place!"

"I'll bet I could write *awesome* scary stories on that old typewriter," I said, staring down at it.

"You want it?" Mrs Carter asked quickly.

"Yes," I answered. "Is it for sale? How much does it cost?"

Mrs Carter motioned with one hand. "Take it," she said.

"Excuse me?" I didn't think I'd heard her correctly.

"Go ahead. Take it," she repeated. "It's yours. For free."

"Do you mean it?" I cried excitedly. "I can have it?"

She nodded.

"Thank you!" I could feel a grin spreading over my face. "Thanks a lot!"

Mrs Carter bent down and picked up something from the floor. "Here," she said. She handed me a fountain pen. A very old-fashioned-looking fountain pen. Heavy and black with silvery chrome on it.

"For me?" I asked, studying the pen.

Mrs Carter nodded again. She smiled at me. "It's my Going-Out-of-Business Special Offer. You get a free pen with every typewriter."

"Wow!" I exclaimed.

Mrs Carter moved to the door and held it open. "Now, get out of here. Both of you," she ordered. "It really is dangerous in here. I'm leaving too."

I hoisted the heavy, old typewriter into my arms. Balancing it against my chest, I followed Alex to the door.

I felt so happy! I thanked Mrs Carter five more times. Then Alex and I said goodbye and headed for our homes.

The street was still wet. It glowed under the street lights like a mirror. It didn't look real.

The walk home seemed to take for ever. The typewriter grew heavier with each step I took.

"Weird," Alex muttered when we finally crossed on to our block.

"Huh?" I groaned. My arms were about to fall off! The typewriter weighed a *ton*!

"What's weird, Alex?"

"The way she *gave* you that valuable typewriter," Alex replied thoughtfully.

"Why is that so weird?" I demanded.

"She seemed so eager to give it away. It's

almost as if she wanted to get *rid* of it," Alex said. She headed towards her house, which is next door to mine.

My knees buckled as I started up my driveway. My arms ached. My whole body ached. I struggled to hold on to the typewriter.

"That's crazy," I muttered.

Of course, I didn't know how right Alex was.

I didn't know that carrying the old typewriter home would totally ruin my life.

I dragged the typewriter into the ranch house where I live. I was gasping for breath. My arms had gone numb.

Mum and Dad were in the living room. They sat side by side on the sofa, doing a crossword puzzle together.

They love crossword puzzles. I'm not sure why. Both of them are terrible spellers. They can never finish a puzzle.

Lots of times, they end up fighting about how to spell a word. Usually, they give up and rip the puzzle to pieces.

Then a few days later, they start a new one.

They both looked up as I lugged the typewriter towards my room.

"What's *that*?" Mum demanded.

"It's a typewriter," I groaned.

"I know that!" Mum protested. "I meant—where did you get it?"

"It's . . . a long story," I choked out.

Dad climbed up from the couch and hurried over to help me. "Wow. It weighs a ton," he said. "How did you ever carry it home?"

I shrugged. "It wasn't so bad," I lied.

We carried it to my room and set it down on my desk. I wanted to try it out right away. But Dad insisted that I return to the living room.

I told them the whole story. About lightning hitting the shop. About going in to explore. About Mrs Carter and how she gave me the typewriter.

I left out the part about the bad electrical shock that knocked me to the floor.

My parents are the kind of people who get upset very easily. I mean, they start yelling and screaming over crossword puzzles!

So I never tell them much. I mean, why ruin their day—or mine?

"Why do you need an old typewriter?" Mum asked, frowning at me. "No one uses typewriters any more. You only see them in antique shops."

"I want to write my scary stories on it," I explained.

"What about your new computer?" Dad demanded. "What about the laser printer we gave you?"

"I'll use that too," I said. "You know. For school work and stuff like that."

Mum rolled her eyes. "Next Zackie will be

writing with a feather quill and an inkwell," she said.

They both laughed.

"Very funny," I muttered. I said good night and hurried down the hall to my room.

I turned the corner that led to my bedroom— and stopped.

What was that strange crackling sound?

It seemed to be coming from my room. A steady, crackling buzz.

"Weird," I muttered.

I stepped into the doorway, peered into my room—and gasped!

"My typewriter!" I cried.

The typewriter was bathed in a bright blue glow. Blue sparks buzzed and crackled off and flew in all directions.

I stared in amazement as the blue current snapped and hummed over the typewriter.

I thought about the shock that had knocked me to the floor in the antique shop. Had the typewriter stored up some of that electricity?

No. That was impossible.

But then why was the typewriter glowing under a crackling, blue current now?

"Mum! Dad!" I called. "Come here! You have to see this!"

They didn't reply.

I hurtled down the hall to the living room. "Quick! Come quick!" I shouted. "You won't believe this!"

They had returned to their crossword puzzle. Dad glanced up as I burst into the room. "How do you spell 'peregrine'?" he asked. "It's a kind of falcon."

"Who cares?" I cried. "My typewriter—it's going to blow up or something!"

That got them off the sofa.

I led the way, running full speed down the hall. They followed close behind.

I stopped at my doorway and pointed to my desk. "Look—!" I cried.

All three of us peered across the room.

At the typewriter. The black metal typewriter with its black roller and rows of black keys ringed with silver.

No blue.

No blue electrical current. No sparks. No crackle or buzz.

Just an old typewriter sitting on a desk.

"Funny joke," Dad muttered, rolling his eyes at me.

Mum shook her head. "I don't know where Zackie gets his sense of humour. Not from *my* side of the family."

"Your side of the family doesn't need a sense of humour. They're *already* a joke!" Dad snapped.

They walked off arguing.

I edged slowly, carefully, into my room. I crept up to the typewriter.

I reached out a hand. I lowered it towards the typewriter.

Lowered it until it was less than a centimetre away.

Then I stopped.

My hand started to shake.

I stared down at the solid, dark machine.

Should I touch it?

Would it shock me again?

Slowly . . . slowly, I lowered my hand.

Alex slammed her locker shut. She adjusted her backpack and turned to me. "So what happened? Did the typewriter zap you?"

It was the next morning. The holidays were over. School had started again.

I had hurried down the hall to our lockers to tell Alex the whole typewriter story. I knew she was the only person in the world who would believe me.

"No. It didn't zap me," I told her. "I touched it, and nothing happened. I pushed down some of the keys. I turned the roller. Nothing happened."

Alex stared hard at me. "Nothing?"

"Nothing."

"That isn't a very good story," she teased. "It has a very weak ending."

I laughed. "Do you think it would be a better ending if I got fried?"

"Much better," she replied.

It was late. The first bell had already rung. The hall was nearly empty.

"I'm going to rewrite the Blob Monster story," I told her. "I have a lot of new ideas. I can't wait to start working on it."

She turned to me. "On the old typewriter?"

I nodded. "I'm going to make the story longer—and scarier. That old typewriter is so weird. I *know* it's going to help me write scarier than ever!" I exclaimed.

I heard giggling.

I spun around and saw Emmy and Annie Bell. They're twins, and they're in our class. Adam came trailing after them. He punched me in the shoulder—so hard, I bounced against the lockers.

Emmy and Annie are good friends with Adam. But not with Alex and me.

They both have curly red hair, lots of freckles, and lots of dimples. The only way to tell Emmy from Annie is to ask, "Which one are you?"

Emmy grinned at me. I mean, I *think* it was Emmy. "Do you really believe in monsters?" she asked.

They both giggled again, as if Emmy had asked something really funny.

"Maybe," I replied. "But I wasn't talking about real monsters. I was talking about a scary story I'm writing."

And then I added nastily, "You two wouldn't

understand—since you haven't learned to write yet!"

"Ha-ha," they both said sarcastically. "You're so funny, Zackie."

"Funny-looking!" Adam added. The oldest joke in the universe.

"But *do* you believe in monsters?" Emmy insisted.

"Adam says you do," her sister added. "Adam says you think a monster lives under your bed!"

"I do not!" I screamed.

They both giggled.

"Adam is a liar!" I cried. I tried to grab him, but he dodged away from me, laughing his head off.

"Zackie sees monsters everywhere," Adam teased, grinning at Emmy and Annie. "He thinks when he opens his locker door, a monster will jump out at him."

They giggled again.

"Give me a break," I muttered. "We're going to be late."

I turned away from their grinning faces. I turned the lock on my locker and pulled open the door.

Then I knelt down to pull out my books.

And something leaped out of my locker!

I saw a white flash.

"Huh?" I cried out in surprise.

Another one jumped out.

And then I gasped when something plopped on to my head.

Something *alive*!

I fell to my knees. Reached up to grab for it.

I felt its claws tangle in my hair.

"Help!" I cried. "Help me!"

The creature moved across my head.

And dropped down the back of my shirt!

Its hot body slid down my skin. Its claws prickled and pinched.

"Help me! Help!" I jumped up, kicking and stomping and squirming.

I frantically slapped at my back.

Adam stepped up to me. He grabbed me by the shoulders. Then he tugged open the back of my shirt.

And plucked the creature off my back.

He held his hand in front of my face. "Wow! What a monster!" he exclaimed. "That's *scaaaaaary!*"

Still trembling, I stared at the creature.

A white mouse.

A little white mouse.

Emmy and Annie were doubled over beside Adam, laughing their heads off.

Even Alex was laughing. Great friend, huh?

"Zackie, I think you really *do* see monsters everywhere!" Annie exclaimed. "Even teeny white ones!"

That got them all laughing again.

"Did you see that awesome dance he did?" Adam asked. Adam did an imitation of my frantic dance. He slapped at his head and neck and stomped wildly on the floor.

"Excellent!" Emmy and Annie declared together.

They all laughed again.

Alex stopped laughing and stepped up beside me. She brushed something off my shoulder.

"Mouse hair," she murmured.

Then she turned to the others. "We should give Zackie a break," she told them. "Someday he's going to be a famous horror writer."

"Someday he's going to be a famous *chicken*!" Annie exclaimed.

Emmy made clucking sounds and flapped her elbows.

"Do you believe it? The famous horror writer is afraid of *mice*!" Adam cried.

Emmy and Annie thought that was really funny. Their red hair bobbed up and down as they laughed.

Emmy glanced at her watch—and gasped. "We're really late!"

She and her sister spun around and ran down

the hall. Adam put the mouse in his pocket and went tearing after them.

I knelt down to pull my books from the bottom of my locker. I reached in carefully. I had to make sure there were no more mice.

Alex stood over me. "You okay?" she asked softly.

"Go away," I snapped.

"What did *I* do?" Alex demanded.

"Just go away," I muttered.

I didn't want her around. I didn't want anyone around.

I felt like a total jerk.

Why did I let little mice scare me like that? Why did I have to freak out in front of everyone?

Because I'm a total jerk, I decided.

I shoved my books into my backpack. Then I stood up and started to close my locker.

Alex leaned against the wall. "I told you to go away," I snapped at her again.

She started to reply, but stopped when Mr Conklin, the principal, turned the corner.

Mr Conklin is a tall, pencil-thin man, with a narrow, red face and big ears that stick out like jug handles. He talks really fast. Always runs instead of walking. And always seems to be moving in eight directions at once.

He eyed Alex, then me. "Who let the mice out of the science lab?" he demanded breathlessly.

"Th-they were in Zackie's locker—" Alex started.

Before she could explain the rest, Mr Conklin narrowed his eyes at me. His face grew even redder.

"Zackie, I'd like to see you in my office," he ordered. "Right now."

I didn't say much at dinner.

I kept wondering if I should tell Mum and Dad about my adventures at school that day. But I decided to keep silent.

I didn't need them laughing at me too.

And I didn't need them asking a million questions about what Mr Conklin said to me.

He had been quite nice about it, actually. He just warned me to try to keep live creatures out of my locker.

After dinner, Dad and I loaded the dishwasher and cleaned up. I was sponging off the dinner table when Alex appeared. "How's it going?" she asked. "Did Mr Conklin—"

I slapped a hand over her mouth to shut her up.

I could see Mum and Dad watching from the other room. "What about Mr Conklin?" Mum demanded.

"He's a nice guy," I replied.

I dragged Alex to the den. "So? How's it going?" she repeated.

"How's it going?" I cried shrilly. "How's it going? How can you ask me 'how's it going'?"

"Well . . ." she started.

"It's going *terribly!*" I cried. "I had the *worst* day! Kids were laughing at me all day. Everywhere I went, kids made mouse faces at me and squeaked at me."

She started to smile, but cut it off.

"I don't know why I lost it like that this morning," I continued. "I felt so dumb. I—"

"It was just a joke," Alex interrupted. "No big deal."

"Easy for you to say," I grumbled. "You didn't have a hundred disgusting rodents crawling all over your body."

"A hundred?" Alex said. "How about *one*?"

"It seemed like a hundred," I mumbled. I decided to change the subject. "Look at this," I said.

I walked over to the desk by the window. After school, I had worked there for three hours. I picked up a stack of pages.

"What are those?" Alex asked, following me to the desk.

"My new Blob Monster story," I replied, holding up the handwritten pages. "I'm making it even scarier."

Alex took the pages from my hand and

shuffled through them. Then she narrowed her eyes at me. "You didn't type them on the old typewriter?"

"Of course not." I took the pages back. "I always write the first draft by hand. I don't type my stories until I've got them just right."

I picked up the pen from the desk. "I used the antique pen that woman gave me in the shop," I told Alex. "What a great pen. It writes so smoothly. I can't believe she gave it to me for free!"

Alex laughed. "You're such a weird guy, Zackie. You get so excited about things like pens and typewriters." And then she added, "I think that's cool."

I glanced over my story. "Now it's time to type it," I said. "I'm so excited. I can't wait to use the old typewriter."

I led the way into my room. I was halfway to my desk when I stopped.

And let out a startled cry.

The typewriter was gone.

Alex and I both gaped at the empty spot on the front of my desktop. Alex pushed up her glasses and squinted.

"It—it's gone," I murmured weakly. My knees started to buckle. I grabbed my dressing table to hold myself up.

"Weird," Alex muttered, shaking her head. "Are you sure—"

"It just disappeared into thin air!" I interrupted. "I don't *believe* this! How? How could it disappear?"

"How could *what* disappear?" a voice called from the doorway.

I whirled around—to see Dad lumber heavily into the room. He carried the old typewriter in his arms.

"Dad—why . . . ?" I started.

He set it down on the desk. Then he pushed his curly black hair off his forehead and grinned at me. "I cleaned it for you, Zackie," he said. "And put in a new ribbon."

He wiped sweat off his forehead with the back of his hand. "Ribbons are hard to find these days," he added. "No one uses typewriters any more."

Alex laughed. "Zackie thought the typewriter had disappeared into thin air!"

I flashed Alex an angry look. "Alex—give me a break," I whispered.

She made a face at me.

Dad shook his head. "It's a little too heavy to disappear into thin air," he sighed. "It weighs a ton! More than a computer!"

I walked over to the typewriter and ran my hand over the smooth, dark metal. "Thanks for cleaning it up, Dad," I said. "It looks awesome."

"A few of the keys were sticking," Dad added. "So I oiled them up. I think the old machine is working fine now, Zackie. You should be able to write some great stories on it."

"Thanks, Dad," I repeated.

I couldn't wait to get started. I reached into my top drawer for some paper. Then I noticed that Dad hadn't left. He was lingering by the door, watching Alex and me.

"Your mum went across the street to visit Janet Hawkins, our new neighbour," he said. "It's such a beautiful spring night. I thought maybe you two would like to take a walk into town to get some ice-cream."

"Uh . . . no thanks," Alex replied. "I had dessert at home. Before I came over."

"And I really want to get started typing my new scary story," I told him.

He sighed and looked disappointed. I think he really wanted an excuse to get ice-cream.

As soon as he left, I dropped into my desk chair. I slid a fresh, white sheet of paper into the typewriter roller.

Alex pulled up a chair and sat beside me. "Can I try the typewriter after you?" she asked.

"Yes. *After* me," I replied impatiently.

I really wanted to get my story typed.

I let my eyes wander over the round, black keys. Then I leaned forward and started to type.

Typing on a typewriter is a lot different from typing on a keyboard. For one thing, you have to press the keys a lot harder.

It took me a few tries to get the feel of the thing.

Then I typed the first words of the story:

IT WAS A DARK AND STORMY NIGHT.

"Hey—!" I uttered a cry as lightning flashed in my bedroom window.

Rain pounded on the glass.

A sharp roar of thunder shook the house.

Darkness swept over me as all the lights went out.

"Zackie—?" Alex cried in a tiny voice. "Zackie? Zackie? Are you all right?"

I swallowed hard. "Yes. I'm okay," I said quietly.

Alex is the only person in the world who knows that I'm afraid of the dark.

I'm afraid of mice. And I'm afraid of the dark.

I admit it.

And I'm afraid of a lot of other things.

I'm afraid of big dogs. I'm afraid of going down to the basement when I'm all alone in the house. I'm afraid of jumping into the deep end of the swimming pool.

I've told Alex about some of my fears. But not all of them.

I mean, it's kind of embarrassing.

Why do I write scary stories if I'm afraid of so many things?

I don't know. Maybe I write better stories because I know what being scared feels like.

"The lights went off so suddenly," Alex said. She stood beside me, leaning over my desk to see out of the window. "Usually they flicker or something."

Sheets of rain pounded against the window-pane. Jagged streaks of lightning crackled across the sky.

I stayed in my desk chair, gripping the arms tightly. "I'm glad Adam isn't here," I murmured. "He'd just make fun of me."

"But you're not very scared now—are you?" Alex asked.

An explosion of thunder nearly made me jump out of the chair.

"A little," I confessed.

And then I heard the footsteps. Heavy, thud-ding footsteps from out in the hall.

Thunder roared again.

I spun away from the window. And listened to the footsteps, thudding heavily on the carpet.

"Who's there?" I called through the darkness. I saw a flicker of yellow light in the doorway. A shadow swept over the wallpaper in the hall.

Dad stepped into the room. "This is so weird," he said. He was carrying two candles in candle-sticks. Their flames bent and nearly went out as he carried them to my desk.

"Where did that storm come from?" Dad asked, setting the candles beside my typewriter. "Are you okay, Zackie?"

I forgot. Dad also knows I'm scared of the dark.

"I'm fine," I told him. "Thanks for the candles."

Dad stared out of the window. We couldn't really see anything out there. The rain was coming down too hard.

"The sky was clear a few seconds ago," Dad said, leaning over me to get a better view. "I can't believe such a big storm could blow in so quickly."

"It's weird," I agreed.

We stared at the rain for a minute or so. Sheets of lightning made the backyard glow like silver.

"I'm going to call your mother," Dad said. "I'm going to tell her to wait out the storm." He patted me on the back, then headed to the door.

"Don't you want a candle?" I called after him.

"No. I'll find my way," he replied. "I have a torch in the basement." He disappeared down the hall.

"What do you want to do now?" Alex asked. Her face looked orange in the candlelight. Her eyes glowed like cat's eyes.

I turned back to the typewriter. "It would be cool to write by candlelight," I said. "Scary stories should *always* be written by candlelight. I'll bet that's how all the famous horror writers write their stories."

"Cool," Alex replied. "Go ahead."

I slid the candlesticks closer. The yellow light flickered over the typewriter keys.

I leaned forward and read over the first sentence of my story:

IT WAS A DARK AND STORMY NIGHT.

Then I hit the space bar and typed the next sentence:

THE WIND BEGAN TO HOWL.

I hit the space bar again. And raised my fingers to type the next sentence.

But a rattling noise made me jump.

"What is *that*?" I gasped.

"The window." Alex pointed.

Outside, the wind blew hard, rattling the windowpane.

Over the steady roar of the rain, I heard another sound. A strange howl.

I gripped the arms of my desk chair. "Do you hear that?" I asked Alex.

She nodded. Her eyes squinted out the window.

"It's just the wind," she said softly. "It's howling through the trees."

Outside, the howling grew louder as the wind swirled around my house. The window rattled and shook.

The howling grew high and shrill, almost like a human voice, a human wail.

I felt a chill run down my back.

Gripping the chair arms tightly, I struggled to keep my fear down.

It's just a storm, I told myself. Just a rainstorm. Just a lot of rain and wind.

I glanced at the words I had typed. In the flickering, orange light, the black type jumped out at me:

THE WIND BEGAN TO HOWL.

I listened to the shrill howl outside. It seemed to surround me, surround the house.

"How strange," I muttered.

And then, things got a lot stranger.

"You're not getting very far with the story," Alex said.

"Well, the storm—" I started.

She put a hand on my shoulder. "You're shaking!" she exclaimed.

"No, I'm not!" I lied.

"Yes, you are. You're shaking," she insisted.

"No way. I'm okay. Really," I said, trying to keep my voice calm and steady. "I'm not that afraid, Alex."

"Maybe if you work on the story, you won't think about the storm so much," she suggested.

"Right. The story," I agreed.

An explosion of thunder shook the house.

I let out a sharp cry. "Why does it seem so close?" I exclaimed. "The lightning and thunder—it sounds as if it's all right in the backyard!"

Alex grabbed my shoulders and turned me to the typewriter. "Type," she ordered. "Pretend there is no storm. Just type."

291

I obediently raised my hands to the keys of the old typewriter. The candles had burned down slightly, and the page was shadowy and dark.

I typed the next sentence:

ALEX AND ZACKIE WERE ALONE IN THE DARK HOUSE, LISTENING TO THE STORM.

Rain pounded hard against the window. In a white flash of lightning, I could see the trees in the backyard, bending and trembling in the howling wind.

"The story is about *us*?" Alex asked, leaning over my shoulder to read what I had typed.

"Of course," I replied. "You know that I always write about us and the other kids at school. It makes it easier to describe everyone."

"Well, don't let the Blob Monster eat me!" she instructed. "I want to be the hero. Not the dinner!"

I laughed.

A crash of thunder made me jump.

I turned back to the typewriter. I squinted to read over the sentences I had typed.

"The candles aren't giving enough light," I complained. "How did writers *do* it in the old days? They must have all gone blind!"

"Let's go and get more candles," Alex suggested.

"Good idea," I agreed.

We each picked up a candlestick. Holding them in front of us, we made our way down the hall.

The candles bent and flickered. Our footsteps were drowned out by the steady roar of rain on the roof.

"Dad?" I called. "Hey, Dad—we need more candles!"

No reply.

We stepped into the living room. Two candles glowed on the mantelpiece. Two more stood side by side on the coffee table in front of the sofa.

"Dad?" I called. "Where are you?"

Holding our candles high, Alex and I made our way to the den. Then the kitchen. Then Mum and Dad's bedroom.

No Dad.

Holding my candle tightly in one hand, I pulled open the door to the basement. "Dad? Are you down there?"

Silence.

I felt another tingling chill run down my back. I turned to Alex. "He—he's gone!" I stammered. "We're all alone!"

"He *has* to be here," Alex insisted. "Why would he go out in this storm?"

"For ice-cream?" I suggested. "He really wanted some ice-cream."

Alex frowned. "Your dad would go out in this storm to get a tub of ice-cream? That's impossible."

"You don't know my dad!" I replied.

"He's here," Alex insisted. She set down the candle and cupped her hands around her mouth.

"Mr Beauchamp? Mr Beauchamp?" she called.

No reply.

Wind howled outside the living-room window. Lightning flickered.

"Hey—!" I cried.

In the flash of bright light, I saw a car in the driveway. Dad's car.

I made my way to the window and peered out. "Dad didn't drive anywhere," I told Alex. "His car is still here. And he wouldn't walk."

"Mr Beauchamp? Mr Beauchamp?" Alex tried again.

"Weird," I muttered. "He wouldn't go out without telling us—would he? He—he's just disappeared."

Alex's eyes flashed. Her expression changed. She narrowed her eyes at me.

"What's wrong?" I asked. "Why are you staring at me like that?"

"Zackie—what was the last sentence you typed?" she demanded, still squinting at me.

"Huh?"

"In your story," she said impatiently. "What was the last sentence?"

I thought hard. Then I recited it:

"ALEX AND ZACKIE WERE ALONE IN THE DARK HOUSE, LISTENING TO THE STORM."

Alex nodded her head solemnly.

"So what?" I asked. "What does the story have to do with anything?"

"Don't you see?" Alex replied. "You wrote that we were all alone in the house—and now we're *all alone!*"

I stared back at her. I still didn't know what she was talking about.

"Zackie—this is amazing!" she cried. "What is the *first* sentence of the story?"

I told it to her:

"IT WAS A DARK AND STORMY NIGHT."

"Yes!" Alex cried excitedly. Her eyes went wide. The candle shook in her hand. "Yes! A dark and stormy night! But it had been a nice night—right?"

"Huh?" I struggled to follow her.

"Your dad said there wasn't a cloud in the sky. Remember? That's why he wanted to walk into town."

"Yeah. Right. So what?" I demanded.

She let out an impatient sigh. "So then you typed that it was dark and stormy—and guess what? It became dark and stormy."

"But, Alex—" I started.

She raised a finger to her lips to silence me. "And then you typed that we were all alone in the dark house. And that came true too!"

"Oh, no!" I groaned. "You're not going to tell me that my story is coming true—are you?"

"So far it has," she insisted. "Every word of it."

"That's really dumb," I told her. "I think this storm has freaked you out more than me!"

"Then how else do you explain it?" Alex shot back.

"Explain it? A big rainstorm started. That's how I explain it."

I picked up a candlestick from the mantel.

Now I had one in each hand. I started back to my room.

Alex followed me. "How do you explain your dad disappearing into thin air?"

Our shadows edged along the wall, bending in the flickering light. I wished the electricity would come back on.

I stepped into my room. "Dad didn't disappear. He went out," I told Alex. I sighed. "Your idea is crazy. Just because I typed that it was stormy out . . ."

"Let's test it," Alex urged.

"Excuse me?"

She dragged me to the desk chair. She pushed me into it.

"Hey—" I protested. "I almost dropped the candles."

"Type something," Alex instructed. "Go ahead, Zackie. Type something—and we'll see if it comes true."

The wind howled outside the house, rattling the windowpane. I set my candles down, one on each side of the old typewriter.

I leaned forward and read the story so far.

Alex was right.

Everything I had typed had come true.

But her idea was totally stupid.

"Type!" she ordered, standing behind me, her hands on my shoulders.

I glanced back at her. "Alex—haven't you ever heard of *coincidence*?"

"Oooh—big word!" she replied sarcastically. "Are you sure you're ready for such a big word?"

I ignored her remark. "A coincidence is when two things happen by accident," I explained. "For example, I type that it's stormy out—and then it starts getting stormy. That's called a coincidence."

She shoved me towards the typewriter. "Prove it," she insisted. "Go ahead, Zackie. Type the next sentence, and let's see if it comes true."

She squeezed my shoulders. And then added, "Or are you *chicken*?"

I wriggled out from under her hands. "Okay, okay," I groaned. "I'll prove just how stupid you are."

I reached for the handwritten pages of the story. And I found the next sentence.

Then I raised my hands to the old typewriter keyboard and typed it in:

THEY HEARD A KNOCK ON THE DOOR.

I lowered my hands to my lap. And sat back.

"See?" I sneered. "Any more bright ideas?"

Then I heard a knock on the door!

I gasped.

Alex let out a startled cry.

"That didn't h-happen," I stammered. "I didn't hear that. I imagined it."

"But we *both* heard it," Alex replied, her eyes wide. "We *both* couldn't imagine it!"

"But it's *impossible*!" I insisted. I picked up a candle. Then I jumped up from the desk chair and hurried across the bedroom.

"Where are you going?" Alex demanded, chasing after me.

"To answer the door," I told her.

"No—!" she gasped.

I was already jogging through the dark hall.

My heart pounded. The candle flame seemed to throb in rhythm with my heart.

I glanced back and saw Alex running after me. "Zackie—wait!"

I didn't stop. I ran to the front door.

"No! Please—don't open it!" Alex pleaded.

"I have to," I told her. "We have to see who's there."

"Zackie—don't!" Alex begged.

But I ignored her. And pulled open the door.

Alex gasped.

I stared out into the rain.

No one there.

No one.

Rain pattered on the front porch. The big raindrops bounced like balls in every direction.

I pushed the door shut. And brushed a cold raindrop off my forehead.

"Weird," Alex muttered, tugging at her blonde ponytail. She pushed her glasses up on her nose. "Weird."

"It had to be a tree branch," I said. "The wind blew a tree branch against the door. That's all."

"No way," Alex insisted. "Tree branches don't *knock*. I heard a knock on the door—and so did you."

We stared at each other for a long moment. Then we stared at the door.

"I know!" Alex declared. Behind her glasses,

her eyes flashed excitedly. "I know why there was no one at the door!"

"I *don't* want to know!" I groaned. "I don't want to hear any more crazy ideas about my story coming true."

"But don't you see?" she cried. "There was no one at the door because you didn't *write* someone at the door!

"*AAAAAGGH!*" I screamed. "Alex, please—give me a break. You don't really believe that I am controlling everything that happens—do you?"

She twisted her face, thinking hard.

"No," she finally replied.

"Good!" I exclaimed.

"I think the old *typewriter* is controlling everything," she said.

"Alex—go and lie down," I instructed. "I'm calling your parents to come and get you. You are *sick*. Definitely sick."

She ignored me. "Maybe that's why the woman in the burned-out shop gave you the typewriter," she continued. "Maybe she knew it had strange powers. And she couldn't wait to get rid of it."

"I can't wait to get rid of *you*!" I snapped. "Alex, please tell me you're not serious. You're scaring me with this nutty talk. Really."

"But, Zackie, I'm right. Everything you type—it comes true!" Alex grabbed *my* arm and started to pull me down the hall.

I pulled back. "Where are you taking me?" I demanded.

"One more test," she insisted.

I followed her into my room. "One more?" I asked. "One more test—and then you'll shut up about this?"

She raised her right hand. "Promise." She lowered her hand. "But, you'll see, Zackie. You'll see that I'm not crazy. Whatever you type on that old typewriter comes true."

I sat down at the desk and slid the candles closer to the typewriter. I stared into the flickering orange light, reading the words of the story.

"Hurry up," Alex urged. "Type that someone is standing on the other side of the door."

"Okay, okay," I muttered. "But this is crazy." I raised my hands to the old typewriter keys and typed:

DRENCHED WITH RAIN, ADAM STOOD ON THE FRONT PORCH.

I lowered my hands to my lap.

I listened for a knock on the front door.

But all I heard was the steady rush of the wind and the patter of rain against the house.

I waited, listening hard.

No knock.

I realized I was holding my breath. I let it out slowly, listening. Listening.

"No knock," I told Alex. I couldn't keep a grin

from spreading across my face. A triumphant grin. "See? It didn't work."

She frowned. She leaned over my shoulder and read the words again. "Of *course* it didn't work," she said. "You didn't write that Adam knocked. You put him on the porch. But you didn't make him knock."

I sighed. "Okay. If it will make you happy . . ."

I turned back to the typewriter and typed:

ADAM KNOCKED ON THE FRONT DOOR.

As I lowered my hands from the keys, I heard a loud knock on the front door.

"See?" Alex cried. It was her turn to grin.

"This *can't* be happening!" I gasped.

We didn't bother with candles. We both ran full speed through the hall to the front door.

Alex reached it first. She grabbed the knob and pulled open the door.

"Is it really Adam?" I called.

I gaped in shock as Alex pulled Adam in from the rain.

He was drenched! His curly black hair was matted to his forehead. He wasn't wearing a kagoule or jacket. His soaked T-shirt stuck to his body.

"Whoooa!" he exclaimed, shivering. He wrapped his arms around his chubby body as if trying to warm himself.

Water poured off him and puddled on the floor.

"Adam—!" I opened my mouth to say something—but I was too shocked to form words.

"It—it's *true*!" Alex stammered. "It really works!"

"Huh?" Adam appeared dazed.

"What are you doing here?" I demanded, feeling dazed myself.

His eyes wandered around the living room.

"I'm not sure!" he exclaimed. "I—I know I came here for a reason. But I don't remember what it is."

"Zackie *made* you come here!" Alex declared.

Adam shook his head hard, shaking water off himself like a dog. He narrowed his eyes at Alex. "Excuse me?"

Alex studied Adam. "Did you stand on the front porch for a while before you knocked?" she demanded.

Adam nodded. "Yeah. I did! I'm not sure why. I just stood there. I guess I was trying to remember why I came over here. How did you know that?"

Alex grinned at me. "See? I was right all along."

I swallowed hard. My head was spinning. "Yes. You were right," I murmured.

The old typewriter . . .

Whatever I typed on it came true.

"What's going on?" Adam demanded impatiently. He shook more water on to the rug. "Why are we in the dark?"

"The storm knocked out the lights," I told him. "Follow me."

I led the way to my room. On the way, I stopped at the linen closet and gave Adam a bath towel. He dried himself off as we walked to my room.

I couldn't wait to tell him about my amazing

typewriter. "You're not going to believe this!" I started.

I took him over to the typewriter. He stared at it in the orange candlelight.

Then Alex and I told him the whole story.

When we finished, Adam burst out laughing. "Very funny," he said.

He shook his head. His curly hair was still soaked. Water dripped down his forehead.

"I know you want to pay me back, Zackie," he said. "I know you want to pay me back for putting the mice in your locker. I know I embarrassed you in school."

He put a moist hand on my shoulder. "But there is no way I'm going to fall for a dumb story like that. No way."

"Zackie will prove it to you," Alex chimed in.

Adam sneered and rolled his eyes. "I can hardly wait."

"No. Really," I insisted. "It's not a joke, Adam. It's real. Come here. I'll show you."

I pulled him up to the desk. Then I dropped into the chair and quickly typed the next lines of my scary story:

THE STORM STOPPED SUDDENLY. ALL WAS QUIET. TOO QUIET.

Adam and Alex read the words over my shoulder.

I jumped up and pulled Adam to the window. "Go ahead. Check it out," I urged.

All three of us slid around my desk and pressed our faces to the window.

"Yes!" I cried, shaking my fists above my head. "Yes!"

The rain had stopped.

I edged between my two friends and pushed up the window. "Listen," I instructed.

We all listened.

Not a sound outside. Not even the drip of rain from the trees. Not even a whisper of wind.

"Yes!" Alex cried happily. She and I slapped a high five.

I turned to Adam. "Do you see?" I cried. "Do you believe us now?"

"Do you see?" Alex repeated.

Adam backed away from the window. "See *what*?" he demanded. "Do I see that the rain has stopped? Yes. I see it."

"But—but—" I pointed to the typewriter.

Adam laughed. "Have you both *lost* it?" he

308

cried. "Do you really think *you* stopped the rain? You two are *totally* messed up!"

"It's true!" I insisted. "Adam, I just proved it to you."

He laughed and rolled his eyes.

I wanted to punch his laughing face. I really did.

Here was the most amazing thing that had ever happened to anyone in the history of the world—and he thought it was a big joke!

I grabbed his arm. "Here," I said breathlessly. "I'll prove it again. Watch."

I dragged him to the typewriter.

I didn't bother to sit down. I leaned over the desk and started to type something.

But before I had typed two words, Alex tugged me away.

"What are you *doing*?" I cried. I struggled to break away. But she pulled me out to the hall.

"He's not going to believe us, Zackie," she whispered. "You can prove it to him a dozen times, and he won't believe it."

"Of course he will!" I insisted. "He'll—"

"No way," Alex interrupted. "Go ahead. Type ADAM HAS TWO HEADS. If you do it, *both* of his heads won't believe you!"

I had to think about that one.

"One more try," I said. "Let me type one more sentence. When Adam sees it come true, maybe he'll change his mind. Maybe he'll see it isn't a joke."

Alex shrugged. "Go ahead. But he has his mind made up, Zackie. He thinks you're trying to pay him back for the mice in your locker."

"One more try," I insisted.

I glanced into the room. "No—! Adam—stop!" I shrieked.

He had his back turned to us. But I could see that he was leaning over the typewriter.

He was typing something on to the page!

"Adam—stop!" Alex and I both wailed.

We leapt into the room.

He spun around, a wide grin on his face. "I've got to go!" he exclaimed.

He swept past us and out into the hall. "So long, suckers!" he called. He disappeared down the hall.

I hurtled to the desk. My heart pounding, I stared down at the typewriter.

What had Adam typed?

I heard the front door slam. Adam had run out of the house.

I didn't care about Adam now. I only cared about one thing.

What had he typed on the old typewriter?

I grabbed the sheet of paper—and pulled it from the roller. Then I held it close to a candle flame to read it.

"Careful! You'll set it on fire!" Alex warned.

I moved it back from the flame. Orange light flickered over the page. My hand was trembling so hard, I struggled to read it.

"Well? What did he type?" Alex asked impatiently.

"He—he—he—" I sputtered.

She grabbed the paper from my hand and read Adam's sentence out loud:

"THE BLOB MONSTER HID IN ZACKIE'S BASEMENT, WAITING FOR FRESH MEAT."

"What a jerk!" I cried. "I don't believe him! Why did he type that on my story?"

Alex stared unhappily at the page. "He thought it was funny."

"Ha-ha," I said weakly. I grabbed the page back from her. "He ruined my story. Now I have to start it all over again."

"Forget your story. What about the Blob Monster?" Alex cried.

"Huh?" A chill tightened the back of my neck. The sheet of paper slipped from my hand.

"Everything typed on the old typewriter comes true," Alex murmured.

I was so upset about Adam ruining my story that I had forgotten!

"You mean—?" I started. My mouth suddenly felt very dry.

"There is a Blob Monster waiting in the basement," Alex said in a low whisper. "Waiting for fresh meat."

"Fresh meat," I repeated. I gulped.

Alex and I froze for a moment, staring at each other in the darting candlelight.

"But there is no such thing as a Blob Monster," I said finally. "I made it up. So how can a Blob Monster be hiding in my basement?"

Alex's eyes flashed behind her glasses. "You're right!" she cried. "They don't exist! So . . . no problem!" She smiled.

But her smile faded when we heard a noise.

A heavy *THUD THUD*.

I gasped. "What was *that*?"

We both turned to the door.

And heard the sound again. *Thud thud.*

Heavy and slow. Like footsteps.

"Is it . . . is it coming from the b-b-b-?" I was so scared I was stuttering.

Alex nodded. "The basement," she whispered, finishing the word for me.

I picked up a candlestick. The light bounced over the wall and floor. I couldn't stop my hand from shaking.

Holding it in front of me, I made my way into the hall.

Alex huddled close, keeping with me step for step.

Thud THUD.

We both stopped. The sounds were closer. Louder.

Taking a deep breath, I stepped up to the basement door.

Alex hung back, her hands pressed to her face. Behind her glasses, her eyes were wide with fear.

THUD THUD.

"It's coming up the stairs!" I cried. "Run!"

Too late.

I heard another *THUD*—and the door crashed open.

A beam of white light made me shut my eyes.

My hands shot up to shield myself.

Behind the beam of light, a large, dark figure lumbered heavily through the door.

"Dad!" I gasped.

My dad lowered the torch to the floor.

"Dad! What were you *doing* down there?" I demanded in a high, shrill voice.

"Are you two okay?" Dad asked, narrowing his eyes at us. "Why do you look so frightened?"

"We . . . uh . . . well . . ." I didn't know how to explain. I *couldn't* tell him we thought he was a Blob Monster!

Dad pointed to the basement with the torch. "I've been down there checking the circuit breakers," he explained. "I can't figure out why the lights haven't come back on." He scratched his head.

"We were looking for you," Alex said. "We shouted down to the basement for you."

"I went across the street to check on your mother. Then I went into the back room of the basement," Dad replied. "I guess I couldn't hear you."

He shook his head. "What a strange storm. It came up so suddenly. And then it just stopped. As if someone turned it on, then turned it off."

Alex and I glanced at each other. "Yes. It was weird," Alex agreed.

I took a deep breath. "Uh . . . Dad?" I started.

He beamed the light at my feet. "Yes, Zackie?"

"Dad . . . when you were down in the basement . . . was there anything else down there with you?"

His heavy eyebrows rose up on his forehead. He stared hard at me. "Excuse me?"

"Did you see anything strange down there? Or hear anything strange?"

He shook his head. "No. Nothing." His eyes locked on mine. "Are you afraid, Zackie? I know you have problems with being in the dark like this. Would you like to stay with me for a while?"

"No. I'm fine. Really," I insisted. "I just wondered . . ."

Dad stepped past us and started towards the kitchen. "I'm going to call the electric company," he said. "They should have fixed the lines by now."

I watched him make his way down the hall. The white beam of light bounced in front of him.

I held my candle up to the basement door. "I guess the typewriter didn't work this time," I told Alex happily. "No Blob Monster."

"Let's go downstairs and find out!" she replied.

"Huh?" I backed away from the open doorway. "Are you crazy?"

"We have to know if the old typewriter has powers or not," Alex said. "We have no choice, Zackie. We have to look in the basement."

"But—but—"

She pushed past me on to the basement stairway. She walked down the first two steps.

Then she turned back to me. "Are you coming with me, or not?"

Did I have a choice?

No.

For one thing, I had the candle. I couldn't let Alex go down there by herself—in total darkness.

But I held back, my heart pounding, my mouth dry as cotton. "Dad said he didn't hear anything," I said. "So there is no reason for us to go."

"That's lame and you know it," Alex replied. She took another step down. "Am I going down alone?"

I forced my rubbery legs to move. "No. Wait. I'm coming," I said.

I lowered my foot to the first stair. "But we'll only stay down for a second—right?"

"Just long enough to see if there is a Blob Monster hiding down there," Alex replied.

Waiting for fresh meat, I added silently.

317

I stumbled on the next step. But caught myself on the railing.

The candle flame dipped low, but didn't blow out.

The basement spread in front of us like a black pit.

We both stopped at the bottom of the steps— and listened.

Silence.

I raised the candle high. Tall stacks of boxes came into view. Behind them, I could see the two wooden wardrobes where Mum and Dad store our winter clothes.

"The Blob Monster could be hiding behind those tall boxes," Alex whispered. "Or in those wardrobes."

I swallowed hard. "Alex—give me a break," I whispered back.

We made our way slowly to the stacks of boxes. I raised the candle high. We peeked behind the first stack.

Nothing hiding there.

"Can we go now?" I pleaded.

Alex rolled her eyes. "Don't you want to know the truth? Don't you want to know if your type-writer really has powers or not?"

"No. Not really," I whispered.

She ignored me. She grabbed the candle from my hand and moved behind the next stack of boxes.

"Hey—give that back!" I cried.

"You're too slow," she snapped. "Keep close behind me. You'll be okay."

"I'm not okay," I insisted. "I want to go back upstairs."

Alex moved quickly between the stacks of boxes. I had to hurry to keep up.

I never liked the basement. In fact, I was afraid of the basement even in the daytime.

I knew there really wasn't anything to be afraid of. But sometimes, telling yourself that doesn't do any good at all.

"Alex—" I whispered. "Can we—?"

I stopped when I heard the sound. A soft slapping, from somewhere against the wall.

Slap. . . slap. . . slap. . . slap . . .

Steady as a heartbeat.

Alex had moved away from me. I saw her walking quickly towards the laundry room.

"Alex—!" I hurtled across the room to her— so fast, I bumped into her.

"Hey—watch it!" she exclaimed.

"Alex—it's down here!" I shrieked. "It's here! It's really here! Listen! Do you hear it?"

We both froze.

The steady, rhythmic sound rose up from the far wall.

Slap...slap...slap...slap...

"Do you hear it?" I whispered.

Alex nodded. Her mouth had dropped open in shock. She gripped the candlestick in both hands.

Slap...slap...

"What are we going to do?" I whispered.

"It's waiting for fresh meat," Alex murmured.

"I know. I know!" I groaned. "You don't have to say it." I pulled her arm. "Come on. We have to tell Dad."

I gazed through the darkness to the stairway. The steps seemed a million miles away.

"We'll never make it," I choked out. "We have to run past the Blob Monster to reach the stairs."

Slap...slap...

"What's our choice?" Alex shot back. "Pick one, Zackie. Choice one: we stay here. Choice two: we don't stay here."

She was right, of course. We had to make a run for it.

Maybe if we ran fast enough, we'd take it by surprise.

Maybe the Blob Monster was too big to run fast.

Slap. . . slap. . . slap. . . slap . . .

"Let's go," Alex urged. "I'll go first since I have the light."

"Uh . . . can we run side by side?" I asked softly.

She nodded.

Without another word, we took off.

Our shoes thudded over the concrete basement floor.

I struggled to keep at Alex's side. My legs felt so heavy, as if I were running uphill!

"Whoooa!" I cried out when the lights flashed on.

Startled, we both stopped running.

I blinked hard, waiting for my eyes to adjust to the bright ceiling light.

Slap... slap ...

We both turned to the far wall to see the Blob Monster.

And stared at a pale white hand slapping against the wall beneath the open basement window.

A *hand*?

Slap... slap ...

"It—it's a rubber glove!" Alex exclaimed.

"It's one of Dad's gardening gloves," I choked out.

Dad usually leaves his heavy gardening

gloves on that window ledge. One of the gloves was hanging from a nail. And the wind kept slapping it against the wall.

Alex laughed first. Then I joined in.

It felt good to laugh. And it felt especially good to know that no Blob Monster was hiding in the basement.

What a relief!

Alex and I climbed happily up the stairs. Then she made her way to the front door. "Thanks for the awesome entertainment!" she teased. "It was better than a movie! See you tomorrow."

She started out the door, then turned back. "We definitely got a little crazy tonight, Zackie. I mean, about that old typewriter."

"Yeah. I guess," I admitted. "It doesn't have any special powers. It didn't make a Blob Monster appear in the basement. And all the lights came back on without me having to type that they came on."

"The typewriter didn't cause *anything* to happen tonight. It was all coincidence," Alex said.

"Oooh. Big word!" I teased.

She slammed the door behind her.

"Are you doing anything, Zackie?" Mum asked.

"Not really."

It was Saturday afternoon, and I was just hanging out. I had a ton of homework to do. So

I was lying on the sofa, staring up at the ceiling, thinking up excuses not to do it.

"Can you run to the shop for me?" Mum asked. "The Enderbys are coming for dinner, and I need a few things." She held up a slip of paper. "It's a short list."

"No problem," I said, climbing up from the sofa.

Maybe I can add a few items to the list, I thought, taking it from her hand. Like maybe a few chocolate bars. Or a box of Pop-Tarts. . .

I love to eat Pop-Tarts raw.

"Ride your bike, okay?" Mum asked. "I'm kind of in a hurry. Come straight back—okay?"

"No problem," I repeated. I tucked the list into the back pocket of my jeans and headed to the garage to get my bike.

The afternoon sun poured down. The air felt hot and dry. More like summer than spring.

I jumped on to my bike and pedalled down the driveway standing up. I turned towards town and sat down, pedalling fast, riding no-hands.

A few minutes later, I leaned my bike against the brick wall of Jack's. Jack's is mainly a butcher's, but they sell fruit, and vegetables, and other groceries too.

The bell over the glass door clanged as I stepped inside. Mrs Jack was at her usual spot, leaning her elbows on the counter beside the cash register.

Mrs Jack is a big, platinum-haired woman with about a dozen chins. She wears bright red lipstick and long, dangling earrings.

She is really nice to everyone—except kids.

She hates kids. I guess she thinks we only come into her shop to steal. When a kid comes in, she follows him up and down the aisles and never takes her eyes off him.

I closed the door behind me and reached into my back pocket for my shopping list.

Mrs Jack had the newspaper spread out in front of her on the counter. She raised her eyes slowly and made a disgusted face at me. "Help you?" she muttered.

I waved the list. "Just buying a few things for my mum."

She grabbed the list out of my hand and squinted at it. Then she handed it back with a grunt. "Tuna is at the back on the bottom," she said.

"Thanks." I picked up a shopping basket and hurried to the back of the shop.

A big air conditioner rattled against the wall. A fan in front of it blew cold air down the narrow aisle.

I found the tuna quickly and dropped two cans into my basket.

The long, white display counter of the meat

department stretched in front of me. Behind the glass, cuts of red meat were lined up in perfect rows.

Beside the counter, an enormous side of beef hung from the ceiling.

That is really disgusting! I thought.

It looked like an entire cow—stripped of its hide—hanging upside down.

Yuck.

I started to turn away from it—when the dead cow moved.

It swung to the right, then swung back.

I stared in surprise.

The cow swung further, to the right, then back.

I watched it swinging on its rope, swinging heavily from side to side.

And then I heard a harsh, whispered voice: "Fresh meat . . . Fresh meat . . ."

"Ohhh." A low moan escaped my throat as I gaped at the side of beef, swinging so slowly, back and forth, back and forth.

"*Fresh meat . . .*" came the raspy whisper again. "*Fresh meat . . .*"

"No—!" I blurted out.

I dropped my shopping basket.

And started to step back.

I let out another cry as Adam stood up and stepped out from behind the meat counter. He had a gleeful grin on his face.

"Fresh meat . . ." he whispered. And burst out laughing.

Annie and Emmy climbed out from behind the counter, giggling and shaking their heads.

"Awesome!" Annie exclaimed.

"Zackie, you're bright red!" her sister laughed. My face burned as hot as the sun. I felt so embarrassed. How could I fall for such a stupid joke?

Now, I knew, they would tell everyone in school that I freaked out over a side of beef!

"What are you *doing* here?" I shrieked.

"We saw you on your bike," Adam replied. "We followed you into the shop. Didn't you see us? We were right behind you."

"*AAAAGH!*" I let out a furious cry and clenched my hands into fists.

"What's going on back there?" Mrs Jack's harsh voice rattled the shelves. "What are you kids doing?"

"Nothing!" I called. "I—I found the tuna!"

I turned back to Adam and the twins. "Give me a break," I muttered.

For some reason, that struck them as funny. They giggled and slapped one another high fives.

Then Adam stuck out both arms. He held them stiffly in front of him, like a sleepwalker. And began marching stiff-legged across the aisle towards me.

"You're controlling me, Zackie!" he declared in a machine-like voice. "I'm in your power."

He staggered towards me like some kind of zombie. "Your typewriter controls me, Zackie. Your typewriter has the power! I am your slave!"

"Adam—you're not funny!" I cried.

The girls giggled. They closed their eyes, stuck out their arms, and started marching towards me too.

"We're in your power," Emmy chanted.

"You're controlling our every move," Annie said.

"This isn't funny!" I shouted furiously. "Get lost, you guys! You—"

I turned and saw Mrs Jack bouncing towards us, her face as red as her lipstick. "What are you doing back here?" she bellowed. "This isn't a clubhouse!"

Adam and the girls instantly lowered their sleepwalker arms. Annie and Emmy backed up against the meat counter.

"Are you buying anything?" Mrs Jack demanded, huffing and puffing from her long journey from the cash register. "If you're not buying anything, get out. Go to the playground."

"We're going," Adam murmured. He couldn't get past Mrs Jack. She filled the aisle. So he scooted down the next aisle.

Annie and Emmy hurried after him.

Mrs Jack glared at me.

"I—I'm almost finished," I stammered. I picked up the basket. I searched for my list, but couldn't find it. No problem. I remembered what was on it.

I found the other items and dropped them into the basket. Mrs Jack stayed with me the whole time.

Then she walked me to the front of the shop.

I paid and hurried out. I was so angry at Adam

and the girls, I forgot all about the chocolate bars.

They are always making fun of me, I complained to myself.

Always playing nasty tricks. Always trying to make me look like a jerk.

Always. Always.

And I'm sick of it. I'm sick to death of it!

"Sick sick sick!" I chanted the word all the way home. I hopped off my bike and let it crash to the driveway. Then I ran inside and tossed the grocery bag on to the kitchen counter.

"Sick sick sick."

I'm going to totally lose it if I don't cool down, I decided.

I ran up to my room and shoved a fresh sheet of paper into the old typewriter.

Then I plopped into the desk chair and furiously started typing. A third Blob Monster story. The scariest one of all. I typed as fast as I could. I didn't think about it. I let my anger do the thinking.

I didn't write it out first. I didn't plan it. I didn't know what was going to happen next.

I leaned over the old typewriter and typed.

In the story, the ugly pink Blob Monster attacks the whole town. People are screaming. Running in every direction. Running for their lives.

Two police officers step forward to fight the

Blob Monster off. It opens its huge mouth—and swallows them whole!

Shrieks of terror fill the town. The enormous Blob Monster is eating everyone alive!

"Yes!" I cried out loud. "Yes!"

I was paying everyone back. Paying the whole town back.

"Yes!"

It was the most exciting, most terrifying story I'd ever written. I wrote page after page.

"Zackie—you forgot something!" a voice called.

I started to type those words into the story. Then I recognized Mum's voice.

Breathing hard, I spun away from the type-writer. I found Mum leaning in the doorway, shaking her head fretfully.

"You have to go back to the shop," she said. "You forgot the loaf of Italian bread. We need bread for dinner tonight."

"Oh. Sorry," I replied.

I glanced back at my story and sighed. It was going so well. I was having such a good time.

I'll get right back to it after I go to the shop, I decided.

I took more money from Mum. Then I picked up my bike from the driveway.

I thought about my Blob Monster story as I pedalled to town. It's the best story I've ever written, I decided.

I can't wait to read it to Alex.

I heard the thud of footsteps on the pavement. A man in a business suit came running by. A dark blur. He ran so fast, I couldn't see his face.

What's *his* problem? I wondered. He's too dressed up to be jogging!

"Whoa!" I had to swerve to the side of the road as a big blue car roared towards me. The woman at the wheel honked her horn and waved frantically at me. Her tyres squealed as she shot around the corner.

"Everyone is in such a hurry today," I muttered to myself.

Then I heard a scream. A man's scream.

I pedalled faster. I was a block from town. I could see the awning over the doorway of Jack's grocery on the corner.

I saw two people running past the shop. Running at top speed, waving their hands.

I screeched to a halt when I heard another scream.

"Look out!" someone shrieked.

"Run! Call the police!"

Two little kids ran past me. One of them was sobbing.

"Hey—what's going on?" I called to them.

But they kept running. They didn't answer.

I started pedalling again; standing up. I leaned over my handlebars, trying to see what all the fuss was about.

As I reached town, I saw people running down the centre of the street. Cars honked. People were screaming.

"Hey—what's going on?" I called. "Is there a fire or something? Hey—somebody tell me what's happening. Somebody—"

And then I *saw* what was happening.

And I opened my mouth in a shrill scream of horror—and fell off my bike.

"OW!"

I landed hard on my right side. The bike slammed on top of me. The handlebar jabbed me in the neck.

A man ran past. "Get away, kid!" he shouted. "Hurry! Get away!"

I shoved the bike off me and climbed to my feet.

My heart pounding in my chest, I brushed myself off.

And gaped at the enormous, pink Blob Monster throbbing on the next corner.

"Ohhh." A horrified moan escaped my throat.

It looks just as I described it in my story! I realized.

Like a huge, slimy human heart. Pink and wet. With tiny black eyes. And purple veins knotted on top of its head. And a mouth cut into its belly.

Throbbing. Throbbing . . .

"It—it's *my* monster!" I cried.

Two little girls frowned at me as their mother tugged them away. I recognized her. Mrs Willow, who lives across the street.

"Zackie—run!" she cried, pulling each girl by a hand. "It's a horrible monster!"

"I know," I murmured.

She pulled her daughters across the street. But I didn't follow them.

I took a deep breath and made my way slowly down the street towards the throbbing Blob Monster.

I wrote this, I realized.

Just before I came to town, I typed this scene. I wrote that the Blob Monster attacked the town.

And I'll bet I know what happens next.

As I stepped closer, I saw the trail of thick slime the monster left behind it. Its belly pulled open, and I saw its purple tongue darting from side to side.

My legs trembled as I stepped even closer.

People screamed and ran. Cars and vans roared past, horns honking.

Everyone was running, desperate to escape. But I couldn't leave. I couldn't take my eyes off it.

I made you! I thought. Horrified and curious and amazed—all at the same time.

I created you!

I wrote this story!

The Blob Monster stared back at me through its tiny, black eyes.

Did it know who I was? Did it know that I'd created it?

As I stared in amazement, its mouth opened wider. It made sick, sucking sounds, and the purple tongue scraped the sides of its mouth.

Thick, yellow drool poured out of the open mouth.

And the Blob Monster bounced forward.

Its purple tongue leaped out at me.

"Hey—!" I cried out. I struggled to back away.

The hot, sticky tongue wrapped around my leg. Started to pull me towards the slimy, open mouth.

"Let go!" I tugged on the tongue as hard as I could. "Help me!"

Two dark-uniformed police officers leaped in front of me. They had their batons raised.

With angry cries, they both began pounding the throbbing creature.

POUND. POUND. POUND.

The batons made a soft plopping sound with each hit.

The Blob Monster uttered a sickening gurgle. And its tongue slid off my leg.

"Run!" one of the officers screamed. "Get going!"

My legs were shaking so hard, I nearly fell. I could still feel the slimy, hot tongue on my leg.

I stumbled back.

And gaped in horror as the Blob Monster pulled open its mouth. The fat purple tongue swung around both police officers.

They beat it with their sticks. They shoved it. They tried to wrestle free.

But the tongue tightened, tightened around them—and pulled them. Pulled them into the huge, open mouth in the creature's belly.

Pulled them both inside.

And then the mouth slammed shut with a disgusting *SPLAT*.

"No! Noooooo!" I wailed.

I wanted to pound my fists against the monster. Pound it until it melted to the ground.

"It's all my fault!" I screamed.

I wrote that scene with the policemen.

It was all in the story I had just typed. I wrote that the Blob Monster ate them both.

And now it had come true!

My frightening story had come true. Every scene of it.

The Blob Monster uttered disgusting gulping sounds as it digested its human meal. Its tiny black eyes locked on mine as it gulped.

What happens next?

What happens next in my story? I asked myself.

Trembling all over, my heart pounding, I struggled to think.

What happens next?

And then—with a shudder—I remembered what I had written.

The Blob Monster follows me home!

The Blob Monster made a final *gulp*. Then it opened its mouth in a disgusting, gassy burp.

Sickened by the sour odour, I staggered back.

I've got to think of something, I told myself. I've got to stop this monster.

Or it will eat me next.

The Blob Monster began to slide forward, plopping wetly on the pavement as it moved.

I knew I couldn't stand there another second. I spun away and forced my rubbery legs to run.

I picked up my bike off the street and jumped on. I began pedalling before I had my balance— and nearly crashed into a brick wall.

I struggled frantically to turn myself around, to calm down enough to ride. Finally, I pedalled away, groaning with each thrust of my foot.

I sped out of town. Halfway down the next block, I glanced back.

Yes. Just as I had written. The Blob Monster was following me. Bouncing rapidly over the pavement. The purple veins on top of its head bouncing with it. Behind it, a trail of slime thickened on the street.

It's so fast! I realized. It's keeping up with me!

What happens next? What did I type next?

"Oh, no!" I shrieked when I remembered.

This is the part where I fall off my bike!

"*AIIIII!*" My front tyre hit a rock—and I went flying over the handlebars.

Once again, I hit the pavement hard. Once again, I shoved my bike off me and jumped to my feet.

I turned to see the Blob Monster catching up. Plopping quickly up the street, its mouth gaping open, its tongue stretching . . . reaching out for me.

I spun away—and ran into Alex and Adam.

"Run! Don't just stand there!" I screeched. "It—it's catching up!"

"Zackie—are you okay?" Alex asked.

"No time for questions!" I gasped, shoving them both. "Run! The Blob Monster is real! I wrote it—and now it's doing everything I wrote!"

Adam laughed. He turned to the Blob Monster. "Do you think I'm stupid, Zackie? This is a joke—right? What is that? Some kind of a balloon?"

"Adam—don't!" I cried.

I grabbed for him. And missed.

He went running up to the Blob Monster.

"Yeah. It's some kind of big balloon!" Adam repeated, grinning.

The monster's purple tongue slid quickly around Adam's waist.

It pulled Adam easily into the open mouth. And then the Blob Monster swallowed him with a sickening *gulp*.

Alex and I both screamed.

Alex turned to me. "Did you write that?" she demanded in a trembling voice.

I nodded. "Yes. It's in my story," I confessed.

Alex grabbed my shoulder. "Well, what happens next? Tell me. What comes next?"

"I—I don't know," I stammered. "That's where I stopped writing!"

Alex and I had never run so fast in our lives. By the time we reached my house, my head was throbbing and my side was aching.

We both gasped for breath as I pushed open the front door. "Anyone home?" I shouted into the house. "Mum? Mum?"

No reply. She must have gone out.

I turned and glimpsed the Blob Monster bouncing hard over Alex's front yard.

"No time!" I cried to Alex. "No time! Hurry!"

She slipped inside the house, and I slammed the door behind us and locked it. Then I lurched towards my room, holding my aching side, forcing my rubbery legs to move.

I mopped the sweat off my forehead with my arm. Then I dropped into the desk chair and raised my hands over the typewriter keys.

Alex hurried up beside me. "What are you going to do?" she asked breathlessly.

"No time to explain," I choked out.

I heard a thumping at the front door. Then I heard a loud *CRAAACK*.

And I knew the huge pink Blob had broken down the door.

"No time. No time!" I declared. I furiously started to type.

"I'm typing an ending," I told Alex. "I'm going to type that the Blob Monster disappears. That it never existed. That Adam and the two policemen are okay."

SQUISSSSH...SQUISSSSH.

Alex and I both gasped. We heard the Blob Monster's slimy body, so close now, moving quickly towards us through the hall.

I knew I had only a few seconds to type the ending.

SQUISSSSSH.

Right outside my bedroom door.

I held my breath and pounded the keys.

Pounded as hard and fast as I could until—

"NOOOOO!"

"What's wrong?" Alex shrieked.

"The keys are jammed!"

We both screamed again as the Blob Monster bounced into the room.

The Blob Monster's body heaved up and down. The creature panted, its entire body bouncing. White slime puddled on the floor around it.

The slash of a mouth in the belly opened and closed, opened and closed. The purple tongue licked the mouth as the monster's eyes narrowed on me.

Alex gasped and backed up against the wall. "Zackie—type the ending!" she screamed breathlessly. "Make that thing disappear!"

"I *can't*!" I cried. I frantically pulled at the keys. "They're jammed. I can't untangle them!"

"Zackie—*please*!" Alex pleaded.

And then I saw the fat purple tongue leap.

It rolled out of the Blob Monster's open belly like a garden hose.

"NOOOOOO!" I opened my mouth in a terrified wail as the tongue stretched across the room. Reached for me . . .

Reached for me . . .

No!

The tongue wrapped around the typewriter. Lifted it easily.

I grabbed for it with both hands.

And missed.

My hands slid across the tongue. So hot. Burning hot. And sticky.

The tongue pulled back, snapped back like elastic. And carried the typewriter into the monster's gaping mouth.

As I stared in horror, the Blob Monster swallowed the typewriter with a single *gulp*.

I leaped up from the desk chair. And stepped up beside Alex. We pressed our backs against the wall and watched helplessly as the Blob Monster throbbed and heaved. Digesting the typewriter.

"We're doomed," Alex murmured. "The typewriter—it's gone. Now there is no way you can destroy the monster."

"Wait!" I cried. "I have an idea!"

I leapt back to the desk. I searched the desktop.

"What are you *doing*?" Alex cried.

The Blob Monster let out sick gurgling sounds as it digested the typewriter. Its body heaved up and down in the puddle of slime it had left on the rug.

"The pen," I told Alex. "The pen—"

I pulled open the desk drawer and saw the old pen in front. I grabbed it and slammed the drawer shut.

I held it up to show Alex. "The old pen the woman gave me. Maybe it has the same powers as the typewriter. Maybe I can write an ending with the pen—and make the Blob Monster disappear!"

"Hurry—!" Alex warned.

The Blob Monster had stopped its gurgling. The purple tongue came darting out again.

I grabbed a sheet of paper and leaned over the desk. I pulled off the cap on the pen and lowered the point to the paper.

"THE—"

I wrote one word—and felt something hot and wet slap against the side of my face.

The fat purple tongue slid against me.

"Ow!" I cried out. And dropped the pen.

My hand shot up to my cheek, and I felt hot, sticky slime.

My stomach heaved.

The tongue curled around the old pen. And carried it to the Blob Monster's mouth.

"Noooo!" Alex and I shrieked together.

The creature sucked the pen into its open belly, and began its digesting gurgles.

"Now what?" Alex asked in a whisper. "What can we do? It's going to eat *us* next!"

I jumped to my feet. The desk chair toppled over.

I stepped away from it, my eyes on the doorway. "Make a run for it!" I cried.

Alex held back. "We can't," she sighed. "That thing—it's blocking the way. We'll never get past it."

She was right. The Blob Monster would stick out its tongue and pull us easily into its drooling mouth.

"Try the window!" I cried desperately.

We both turned to the window.

No way. It was bolted shut because of the air conditioner.

"Doomed," Alex whispered. "Doomed."

We both turned back to the throbbing, pink monster.

And then I had one more idea.

"Alex—remember when Adam typed something on my story? And it didn't come true?"

She nodded, keeping her eyes on the gurgling Blob Monster. "Yes, I remember. But so what?"

"Well," I continued, "maybe that's because it's *me* that has the power. Maybe the power isn't in the typewriter or the pen. Maybe I got the power that night in that antique shop when I was zapped by that electrical shock."

Alex swallowed hard. "Maybe . . ."

"Maybe it's been in *me* the whole time!" I cried excitedly. "All I have to do is *think* what I want to happen—and it will come true. I don't have to type it or write it. I just have to *think* it!"

"Maybe . . ." Alex repeated.

She started to say something else. But the Blob suddenly bounced forward, squishing over the rug. And its tongue rolled out towards us.

"Ohhhh . . ." Alex backed up against the wall.

The fat tongue licked her arm. It left a thick smear of sticky drool on her skin.

"Think fast, Zackie!" Alex cried.

The tongue curled and started to wrap itself around Alex.

"Make it disappear!" Alex pleaded. "Think! Think it away!"

I froze in horror as the fat tongue wrapped around Alex. It lifted her off the floor.

Screaming, she thrashed her arms and kicked. Squirming frantically, she wrapped her hands around the sticky tongue—and shoved with all her strength.

But the disgusting tongue squeezed tighter, held her in its slimy grip.

I shut my eyes.

Think! I instructed myself. Think *hard*!

Think that the Blob Monster is gone.

Gone . . . gone . . . gone.

I held my breath. And thought with all my might.

Would it work?

The monster is gone.

That's what I thought.

The monster is gone . . . gone . . . gone . . .

I silently chanted the word, over and over. Then I opened my eyes.

And the Blob Monster was gone!

Alex stood in the centre of the floor, a dazed expression on her face. "It . . . it worked," she choked out.

I *do* have the power! I realized.

I closed my eyes again and started to think. *Adam is back*, I thought.

Adam is back . . .

I opened my eyes—and Adam stood beside Alex.

He blinked several times, then squinted at me. "What's happening?" he asked.

"I have it!" I cried happily. "I have the power—not the typewriter!"

"What are you *talking* about?" Adam demanded. "What power?"

I shook my head. "You wouldn't understand," I told him.

Alex started to laugh.

Before I realized it, I was laughing too.

Joyful laughter. Relieved laughter.

All three of us stood there, laughing, laughing, laughing—laughing happily ever after.

"Well? Did you like my story?"

The pink Blob Monster neatened the pages he had just read and set them down on the desk. He turned to his friend, a green-skinned Blob Monster.

"Did you just write that?" the green monster asked.

The pink Blob Monster gurgled with pride. "Yes. Did you enjoy it?"

"I did," his friend replied. "Thank you for reading it to me. It's very exciting. Very well written. What do you call it?"

"I call it 'Attack of the Humans'," the Blob Monster replied. "Did you really like it?"

"Yes. Those humans are really gross," his friend replied. "Do you know my favourite part?"

"What part?"

"When the Blob Monster ate Adam. That was really fun!" the green creature declared. "But I have just one problem with your story."

352

The pink Blob Monster bobbed up and down. The veins on top of his head turned a darker purple. "A problem with my story? What is it?"

"Well . . ." his green friend replied. "Why did you give it such an unhappy ending? I hated it when the human shut his eyes, and the Blob Monster disappeared. That was so sad."

"Do you think so?" the pink monster asked, gazing down thoughtfully at the pages he had written.

"Yes," his friend replied. "You should have a happy ending, instead. Everyone likes a happy ending."

The pink Blob Monster picked up his story. "Okay. You're right. I'll change the ending. I'll have the Blob Monster eat them all!"

"Great! I love it!" his friend declared. "Now, *that's* a great ending!"

Reader beware – we're counting down to a scare!

 **THREE** completely new Goosebumps titles in one book…

 **TWO** hard covers which make it the first EVER Goosebumps hardback…

 **ONE** weird wailing chip that'll make you jump out of your skin…

 **LIFT-OFF!** It's the **GOOSEBUMPS WAILING SPECIAL,** blasting into a bookshop near you. Don't be the only one to miss take-off…

R.L.Stine

Reader beware, you're in for a scare!

These terrifying tales will send shivers up your spine:

Goosebumps

Reader beware – here's THREE TIMES the scare!

Look out for these bumper GOOSEBUMPS editions. With three spine-tingling stories by R.L. Stine in each book, get ready for three times the thrill … three times the scare … three times the GOOSEBUMPS!

Reader beware – you choose the scare!

Give Yourself Goosebumps

A scary new series from R.L. Stine – where
you decide what happens!

Choose from over 20 scary endings!

HIPPO GHOST

Summer Visitors

Emma thinks she's in for a really boring summer,
until she meets the Carstairs family on the beach.
But there's something very *strange* about her
new friends. . .

Carol Barton

Ghostly Music

Beth loves her piano lessons. So why have they
started to make her *ill*. . . ?

Richard Brown

A Patchwork of Ghosts

Who is the evil-looking ghost tormenting Lizzie,
and why does he want to hurt her...?

Angela Bull

The Ghosts who Waited

Everything's changed since Rosy and her family
moved house. Why has everyone suddenly
turned against her. . .?

Dennis Hamley

The Railway Phantoms

Rachel has visions. She dreams of two children
in strange, disintegrating clothes. And it seems
as if they are trying to contact her...

Dennis Hamley

The Haunting of Gull Cottage
Unless Kezzie and James can find what really happened in Gull Cottage that terrible night many years ago, the haunting may never stop...
Tessa Krailing

The Hidden Tomb
Can Kate unlock the mystery of the curse on Middleton Hall, before it destroys the Mason family...?
Jenny Oldfield

The House at the End of Ferry Road
The house at the end of Ferry Road has just been built. So it can't be haunted, can it...?
Martin Oliver

Beware! This House is Haunted
This House is Haunted Too!
Jessica doesn't believe in ghosts. So who *is* writing the strange, spooky messages?
Lance Salway

The Children Next Door
Laura longs to make friends with the children next door. But they're not quite what they seem. . .
Jean Ure